fine.

BIANCA K. GRAY

contents

WHEN I WAS MURDERED, the first person that I thought of was Jayden King. Not for any sentimental reasons, but simply because if anyone was going to murder me, it had to be him.

Unfortunately, I have known Jayden King since Mrs. Viper's sixth grade English class. While we were learning how to diagram sentences, Jayden King was memorizing basketball plays. And it worked out for him, as he is now on his way to becoming a basketball legend like his father, James King. You may be thinking, why would a professional basketball player want to murder *you*? The answer to that is a long story.

"Grace!" my best friend since elementary school shouted out through my headset as I tried to aim the gun my avatar was holding. I jumped from the sound and, almost immediately after, my avatar died. I pressed the button to respawn, annoyed, as I greeted my friend.

"Hey Will," I said, as I started smashing buttons in order to shoot at my opponent.

"Happy birthday," Will cooed, causing an eyebrow of mine to raise.

"Please don't tell me—"

"Hey G," a low voice echoed. I checked who entered my party and I was right. *Basketballboy97*, otherwise known as Jayden King, maker of the most basic usernames to ever exist. I felt my eyes roll to the back of my head.

"He wanted to play before the game," Will explained. Will and I were neighbors our whole lives. His mom was the only person in the cul-de-sac to welcome my Korean mother into the neighborhood. Shortly after Mrs. Pearson became close to my mom, Will and I naturally became fast friends. We were inseparable growing up and it was just us two. That is until middle school started.

Middle school put together the three elementary schools in the area, connecting Will and I to a larger group of people that we've never met before. I didn't speak to anyone in the sixth grade, while Will was the most talkative I had ever seen him. He joined the basketball team, and made a *huge* group of friends that he, luckily, introduced me to. But, the worst day of my life was when I went over to Will's house to see Jayden King and him playing the video game Crash Team

Racing. The game that Will and *I* always played together.

I didn't necessarily *hate* Jayden King at this point. I thought he was an arrogant, annoying, *jackass* but I didn't hate him. That bit came later. But ever since the sixth grade, Will has been great friends with Jayden King, which meant I had to tolerate him on some level. I just didn't think he would follow me into adulthood.

"You still living in New York?" Jayden's voice asked. I removed part of my headset so that it was only on one ear. Jayden's voice was always way too loud.

"Can you stop breathing into the mic?" I asked, annoyed.

"Can you stop making shit calls?" Jayden retorted, referring to my job. I couldn't help but roll my eyes again.

"Hey, it's Grace's birthday," Will said, trying to mediate between the two of us, as per usual.

"Oh happy birthday," Jayden said, absentmindedly.

"Shouldn't you be getting ready for the game?" I asked, as I died again. I sighed, frustrated, as my fist hit the desk. I sucked at first person shooter games.

"Shouldn't you?" Why he always answered my questions with a question, I would never know. I glanced over at the time. He was right, annoyingly. It *was* almost time for me to get ready.

"Better not make dumbass calls tonight," Jayden warned.

"If you get in my face tonight, Jayden, I swear to God I'll kick you out of the game," I threatened.

"I feel like that would be a biased call, don't you think Will?" Jayden said and I swore I could hear the mischievous smile in his voice. At his words, I shut my mouth and took off my headset. Exiting the game, I muttered curses at Jayden. No one in my profession knew that I knew him as well as I did. If they *did* know, I probably wouldn't be able to officiate his games or maybe I wouldn't have been able to be a part of the league at all. And being a referee in the NBA was a dream of mine come true.

Putting on the white and black striped shirt over my black pants, I looked at myself in the mirror. This was the first year that I was working for the NBA and I wanted the year to go perfectly. But, I couldn't help but hear Jayden's voice echo in my head. *Can you stop making shit calls?*

A knock on the door shook me out of my thoughts, and I opened the hotel room door to reveal Valentina Sanchez, the only other female referee in the NBA.

"Mama, *what* is going on with your hair?" she called out, her hazel eyes wide upon seeing me. She walked into the room as she grabbed my ponytail and dragged me into the bathroom.

"This game is going to be televised on ESPN, do you realize that?" she asked as she pulled my ponytail apart and then started brushing like a mad woman. I stared helplessly into the mirror at her. Her hair was pulled into a sleek ponytail with her baby hairs framing her oval-shaped face perfectly and I could see that she was about to do the same kind of hair style on me. I pulled my head away from her hands as she finished pulling my black hair into a neat ponytail.

"It's fine," I said. "No one is looking at me anyways. They're paying attention to the game, not the refs."

"Do you want to give them something else to cuss you out over?" she pointed out as she looked into the bathroom cabinets for something.

"*Dios mio*, do you not own a curling iron?" she asked, her eyes glancing over at me desperately. I shrugged.

"I don't really know how to use one," I muttered quietly.

"There's YouTube, Grace," she said, throwing her hands up. "It's called learning a new skill." She was right. I had no excuse. But, I hated people looking at me. And changing up my style always made me feel like people were staring at me, even if they weren't. I ducked my head away from Valentina's prying hands.

"It's fine," I said, again. "I like how my hair looks. You put it into a nice ponytail." Valentina smiled slightly at the compliment.

"Just because we like sports doesn't mean we can't be girly," she said. I nodded in timid agreement.

"I know," I responded. I *did* know. But, it was hard to get over some of that internalized misogyny that I had picked up throughout the years. Growing up with boys who seemed to hate everything about women made it hard for me to embrace the feminine side of me. Instead, it made me want to repress it to the point of oblivion. I admired Valentina because she grew up with the same comments and yet still embraced that side of her wholeheartedly.

"You're from this area, aren't you?" Valentina asked as she fixed part of her hair in the mirror.

"Yeah, kind of," I said. "I'm from outside of D.C. But my dad, actually, has always been really into basketball and he's going to be here tonight."

"Oh that's fun! Just your dad?" Valentina asked. I nodded slowly. I hadn't known Valentina for long, though we did run into each other when we were officiating college teams. Because we had just become friends, she didn't know much about my family.

"Yeah," I muttered, not knowing what I should say or what I should leave out. "Uh, my brother is busy with his baby so he can't come."

"What about your mom?" she asked. I felt a weight start to settle in my chest.

"Uh," I started, eventually deciding to just tell her everything, "Um, she passed away." Valentina's head turned so that she could look at me head on, her eyes wide.

"I'm so sorry," she said, quietly. "How did it happen?"

"Oh, she had brain cancer," I answered, trying to swallow the lump that was forming in the back of my throat. "She died when I was seventeen."

"I'm so, so sorry, Grace," she said. She pulled me

into a hug and I sat there, surprised. I wasn't one that liked this kind of comfort; the hugging. Physical touch wasn't something that I enjoyed. But Valentina's hug was nice and felt genuine.

"It's fine," I said, pulling myself out of the hug. "I'm okay. It's been *years*. I'm over it." I wasn't and was never going to be, but I didn't want to linger on the topic for too long. Valentina looked down at her watch and her eyebrows raised.

"Let's go," she said, clapping her hands together. The moment, gone. "We can't be late or he'll kill us." Valentina was referring to the other referee who was working with us tonight. Charles Johnson was a veteran while Valentina only had a couple of years working for the league and I was new. He was the type to lecture and I didn't want to be lectured *again* by Charles.

I quickly put on my running shoes and grabbed my hotel room key. Valentina and I ran as fast as we could down the hotel halls and down the steps, running into Charles in the lobby. Charles was incredibly tall, almost as tall as the other basketball players. He played ball in college but never quite made it to the NBA, becoming a referee instead.

"If you two got here a minute later, we'd be having some words," Charles warned. Valentina and I gave each other a knowing glance before following Charles out.

two

MY SHOES SQUEAKED against the court floor as I inspected the basketball that was going to be used. As I felt the basketball's weight and air pressure with my hands, a looming shadow fell over me. I threw my head backwards to look up at the shadow and then rolled my eyes at the sight.

"You gonna be fair tonight?" Jayden asked, walking into my peripheral vision.

"I'm fair every night," I retorted, looking back at the basketball in my hands.

"You're not," Jayden pointed out. "You target me the most." A dry chuckle escaped my lips.

"I don't target you the most. You're just the worst at following the rules," I said, finally turning my attention to him. My eyes widened at his facial expression. Jayden looked more... frustrated than usual. His face looked dark, somehow.

"I'm not the only official that calls you out on your

—" I started to say in order to defend myself, but he wouldn't let me finish.

"Listen, I'm really not in the mood tonight. This game's really important for me," he muttered. I felt my face soften as his eyes focused on someone behind me.

"Just don't be on my ass tonight," Jayden warned. His brown eyes emphasized that message as they met mine before he walked away. I rolled my eyes as Valentina walked up to my side, her eyes lingering on Jayden's back.

"You guys know each other?" she asked. I felt my ears burn as I shook my head.

"No," I lied, "We've just had a lot of bad experiences together on the court." Her eyes met mine for a second and then she laughed.

"Yeah, I've seen the clips of him arguing with you," she laughed as she said it. I glared at the back of Jayden's head. If I dared to call too many fouls on him, he would always get into my face and argue at some point during the game. I stared at him as he walked back into the locker room. I was never scared when Jayden argued aggressively at me. It was something I had gotten used to as I would officiate his games throughout high school and college. And I never thought he would hurt me, at any point. But today—Jayden's face flashed through my mind—there was something about him that scared me today. I pulled my eyes away from Jayden's figure, as he turned the corner, and tried to smile at Valentina.

"Those clips are the best," I said sarcastically. She laughed again as Charles came up to us.

"Did you guys check the equipment, the ball, the timer, everything?" he asked. We both nodded our heads as he ignored our answer and went on to double check the equipment.

"You're not the only ref he argues with though," she said, putting an arm around me as we went to go wait for the game to start. She was right. At least he was consistent.

"Oh, Grace," a lanky brunette said, running up to Valentina and I. I glanced down at the envelope in his hands.

"Hey Greg," I said slowly. Greg worked at the stadium as one of the guys who wiped the sweat off of the court as the game went on. We had talked a couple of times but didn't know each other super well. All I knew about him was his name and that he *seemed* nice. But, all men seemed nice at first.

"I remember you mentioned once that today was your birthday, so I got you a card," he said, running his hands through his shaggy brown hair. "Happy birthday." His green eyes met mine for a second and then looked away quickly as he held out the card. Valentina's eyes were boring holes into my face.

"Oh, uh, thanks Greg," I stammered, taken aback, as I took the card from his hands. The stadium was starting to fill up with fans and the two teams were about to come out for warm ups. Greg looked like he wanted to say something, but instead quickly turned around and walked over to the other side of the court.

"A birthday card?" Valentina asked as her eyebrows raised. I shrugged as I went to put it in my bag.

"He's a nice guy," I said, scanning the crowd for my dad. I knew I wasn't going to be able to find him, as he insisted on paying for his own ticket and the stadium was massive, but I tried anyway.

"He might like you," Valentina pointed out. I scrunched up my face.

"What's that face for?" Valentina asked. "Wait, don't tell me you don't date." I shrugged, trying not to make eye contact.

"It's not that I don't date. I just have... neverdatedbefore," I said the last part of my sentence quickly and under my breath. Valentina raised her eyebrows.

"Sorry, what did you say?"

"Ineverdatedbefore," I mumbled.

"Yeah, say that one more time," she said, leaning in towards me. I took a deep breath.

"I've never dated before, Val," I whispered, a bit angrily due to the embarrassment. It was humiliating to admit to people that I had never been on a date or had a boyfriend before. I had never even had my first kiss and I was twenty-four years old. It was way past the time to have done these things.

Valentina's eyes widened as she stared at me in shock. Her jaw was slightly open a bit and my hand tapped her chin so that she would close it.

"*Grace!*" she exclaimed.

"What?" I asked, sheepishly.

"You're twenty-four!" she whisper-yelled. I nodded my head slowly.

"I know," I muttered.

"How have you—I mean, how???" Valentina asked, clearly in disbelief. She took a couple of steps back and looked me up and down. "You have a *great* body and you're not ugly."

"Thanks," I mumbled, even though I knew I looked like a cardboard standee. I shrugged. "I don't know. I just have never dated before. No one has really asked me out and I'm more focused on... other things."

"No one has asked you out?" she asked, incredulously. I thought back to every time I talked to a boy.

"Well, not *seriously*," I said. "I just don't really talk to boys except my best friend from childhood and—" I was about to say Jayden but stopped myself.

"And... casual encounters with boys but that's about it," I finished the sentence. I hoped that Valentina wouldn't notice the pause but nothing really escaped her. I watched a manicured eyebrow raise, but she didn't ask.

"Did you not go out during college?" Valentina asked. I shook my head.

"I don't really like going out to bars and clubs, and besides, I was busy studying," I said.

"Studying what?" she asked.

"I would watch recorded games to see where

there's a foul and everything," I said. She threw up her hands.

"Grace, there's more to life than just basketball," she pointed out.

"I know," I said quietly. Before she could lecture me anymore, Charles motioned for us to get into position. The game was about to start. As Valentina walked away, she gave me a look that said: *This conversation isn't over.* I mentally prepared myself for the questioning that was going to come after the game.

As I walked over to my place, I watched as Jayden walked out of the stadium for one final talk with the coach before he had to come in when his name was announced. His face was dark, the darkest I had ever seen it. His brown eyes darted over at me, and he glared before I turned away. I didn't know what was going on with him, but it didn't concern me. I was going to do my job, and I didn't care if Jayden King got upset about it.

three

"TRAVELING," I called out, moving my hands in a circular motion. "On number 23." I used my fingers to demonstrate the number so that the scoreboard could see it. An announcer called out the foul to the groan of many in the crowd. Jayden threw the ball hard at me, and I barely caught it. It was his third foul.

"I wasn't traveling," he said as he stalked past me. I rolled my eyes. At least he wasn't arguing, yet. That usually started happening on his fourth foul. I threw the ball to the other team and started running with the players. My breathing quickened as I moved my legs hard in order to keep up with the massively tall players. It was almost the end of the third quarter and my legs were starting to feel like jelly. Jayden's team, the Washington Wolves, were ahead by 12 points. It looked like they were going to win.

I watched as Jayden jumped up to defend, but he

clearly jumped at an angle, knocking the ball out of the other player's hands.

"Blocking foul," the announcers said over the speaker, after I made the call, "On number 23." His fourth foul. If looks could kill, I would be dead right now. Jayden walked over and leered down at me.

"I jumped perfectly straight, *ref*," he spat out.

"You didn't," I muttered. "It was clear as day. That was a blocking foul."

"I told you I'm not in the mood tonight," he said, getting angry.

"I'm not targeting you."

"You make shit calls and you're a terrible fucking ref," he yelled out before walking away. I turned slightly to his coach.

"Coach, you better get your player under control," I said, my blood starting to boil. Charles threw the ball to the other team and the game started again. I tried to avoid looking at Jayden so that I wouldn't see all his fouls, but he always had the ball. He was really great at shooting, but was always cutting corners when he was defending. I watched as he grabbed the player with the ball and immediately blew my whistle. Jayden was just fucking up left and right today.

"Holding," I called out, "On number 23." I said the last part a little dejectedly. It was his fifth foul. Jayden glared at me.

"Are you *kidding* me, Grace?" he exploded.

"Coach," I called out.

"I *asked* you not to target me tonight, pretty politely too," he hissed.

"I'm doing my job," I snapped back. "Maybe if you would just do yours, you wouldn't be getting fouls tonight. Your team is *up*. Chill *out*, Jayden." His long index finger pushed my shoulder as I glared up at him.

"Don't tell me what to do, Lee," he spat.

"If you touch me again, I'm ejecting you," I hissed.

"It looks like you're going to eject me anyways," he glowered.

"King, King, *get over here*," his coach called. The coach took Jayden out of the game, replacing him with another player. I felt Jayden's glare on my back the entire time as I ran back and forth on the court. Sweat covered my entire body. I trained for months for my body to be in good enough shape to keep up with these guys, but it was still tiring.

The other team was starting to rack up points, the difference between the Wolves and them only being 4 points. Because of this, Jayden was put back into the game. He only had one more foul before he would be ejected from the game, and he glared at me as he took his place back onto the court. Despite the threat that lay behind his eyes, I wasn't worried. He hadn't ever been ejected from a game before. Not in all the years that I've known him. He had anger issues, for sure, but he always calmed down enough to the point where the foul before he got ejected was the last foul that he would make in the game. He wouldn't make another mistake. But, as I looked at the heat rising from his body, the glower that graced his delicate features, a part of me felt *slightly* worried.

The game started up again and it was almost the end of the fourth quarter. The game was close, only a two point difference between the two teams. When one would score, the other team would too. And I could see the tension building up in Jayden's body. *Why is this game so important to him?* It wasn't like this game was the play-offs or the finals.

It was down to the last minute of the game and the other team had tied it up. The Wolves had taken a time out but were back on the court again. And it was almost as if I were watching the whole thing in slow motion. Jayden had the ball. He was flying down the court and was going in for a lay-up. And I watched as he committed his final foul. The foul before being ejected from the game. In a split second, I had to decide if I should call it or not, but it was *such* an obvious foul. He hit the defender in the chest. I stared at him as he quickly made the shot, but I blew my whistle anyway.

"Charging," I muttered, "On number 23." Jayden's eyes met mine and I don't think I had ever seen him so angry. I felt myself tremble from fear as he threw the ball to Valentina. He didn't even yell at me, it was just a quiet anger as he stalked off of the court. But, I almost wished he would yell at me. How he was acting felt much worse. His look chilled me to the bone.

The Wolves lost the game without their star player. And I knew that Jayden was not going to speak to me for a while and I was going to have to hear about it inevitably from Will later. I watched as Jayden walked back to the locker room, his eyes avoiding mine. Biting the inside of my cheek, I almost didn't realize that Greg was standing in front of me, until he moved so that he was blocking my vision of Jayden.

"Hey, Grace," he said.

"Hi," I said, trying to not look past him in order to follow Jayden with my eyes. I was failing at it. I closed my eyes and then tried to smile at Greg.

"Sorry," I muttered. "Rough game." Greg nodded.

"Yeah, I saw that whole thing with King," he said. "He gets angry with everyone I think." I nodded my head. Greg stared at me for a moment and I shifted uncomfortably in his gaze.

"Yeah, so," he said, looking down at the ground, "I was wondering if you wanted to—" Jayden popped out of the locker room just to glare at me, childishly, and then walked back into the locker room.

"Sorry, Greg," I said, tightening my lips into a thin line. "I have to go."

"Oh, okay," I heard Greg mumble as I walked past him. As I walked out of the stadium, I grabbed my bag and slipped into one of the restrooms. I changed my shirt, stuffing my referee one into my bag, angrily. My thoughts stayed on Jayden. *What was he so pissed about? He* was the one who kept making the fouls. *I* was just doing my job.

Staring myself down in the mirror, my eyes glanced over the parts of my face that I hated the most; the smallness of my eyes, the shortness of my forehead, the roundness of my features. Frustrated, I pulled the hair-tie out from my dark hair, letting it fall over my shoulders as I placed the hair-tie in my mouth. Pulling it all back up, I put it in a quick, messy bun and walked out of the bathroom, my bag slung over my shoulder.

Jayden's betrayed eyes forced its way back into my brain and I felt tears start to prick at the corners of my eyes. *It wasn't fair.* Why did I even care what he thought about me? I reached for my cell phone in my bag and looked at the blinking notifications. One was from my father telling me that it might take him a while to meet me outside of the stadium. The other was from my therapist asking if I was okay since he watched what happened during the game. I quickly texted my father, "Okay" and then hit the green call button on my therapist's number.

Dr. Elijah Adler. He had been my therapist ever since my mother was diagnosed with cancer. Even though my mother was firmly against me seeing a therapist, as it was considered an embarrassment to seek help with mental health issues in Korean culture, my father encouraged it as he grew up in America. He thought it would help me deal with the fact that my mother had stage IV brain cancer.

During this time, Dr. Adler was a huge help. He was close to my age, only being around his mid-twenties when he first started treating me. He understood me and didn't seem to judge me with his calculating ice-gray eyes, as I thought a therapist would. If he wasn't my doctor, I would've considered him a friend of mine. He knew things about me that even Will didn't know.

"Grace," his voice was like steel. It was always at the same level in the same tone. The consistency of how he sounded was a comfort to me.

"You saw the game?" I asked as I leaned against the wall of the stadium. I looked up at the dark sky, hoping to catch a glimpse of some stars in this city. I didn't see any.

"I did. I wanted to reach out in case you were feeling... uncomfortable," he said. He meant unstable.

"I'm fine," I barely mumbled. Dr. Adler was quiet on the other end, but I could hear him lightly breathing.

"You've been bothered by Jayden King a lot lately," he simply said. I scrunched my thin eyebrows together.

"I don't know what you mean," I said, feeling myself get frustrated at the mention of his name.

"You've been bringing him up a lot during our recent sessions," he said. "I thought we moved past Jayden." After my mother died, during our therapy sessions, I would mention Jayden a lot. Whether he annoyed me that day, or why he seemed to hate me that day, or this and that. Just constantly, I was consumed by the thought of Jayden and how much he annoyed me or bothered me. Dr. Adler said it was to the point of obsession.

I picked at the sweater I was wearing. It was almost winter, but the weather around D.C. was always fickle. Today, it was still warm enough to wear a light sweater.

"Grace?"

"I'm fine," I said, again. A mantra that I would say to myself constantly in order to repress whatever feeling was bubbling up. "I'm just annoyed with him because he just seemed more upset than usual about my calls, that's all." I heard Dr. Adler take a sharp breath, almost like he was angry with me.

"We don't want to waste our emotions on a guy like him, do we?" he said. His voice was still even, though there was something behind his tone that made my blood chill.

"No, I know," I muttered.

"I will ask to up your dosage," Dr. Adler said. "We don't want you to have more anxious thoughts over Jayden King."

"He just scares me, sometimes," I said, quietly, seeing my father exit the stadium. His head full of black-gray hair was swiveling around, looking for me.

"If he ever touches you, he will pay for it," Dr. Adler said, his voice still the same, though his words spoke of a threat.

"I have to go," I said. "My father's here." I hung up on Dr. Adler, something that he hated me doing. But, I didn't want to listen to his assumptions. I wasn't scared of Jayden because I thought he would hurt me. I was simply just scared of him. As to why, I wasn't sure.

four

"GRACE!" my father called out, once he locked eyes with me. He waved his arms over his head. I stuffed my phone into my back pocket and hurried over to him as he zipped his jacket up. Daniel Lee was not an average, stereotypical Asian dad. He was incredibly animated, extremely laid-back, and loved basketball more than anything. He grew up watching the games on TV and had this dream of one day playing for the NBA. Unfortunately, Daniel Lee, otherwise known as Sang-hoon, grew up to only be five foot nine so his dreams of playing professional basketball were dashed. Despite this, Daniel was still running around on various courts in Northern Virginia playing pick up basketball with anybody who would dare play with him.

"I think you made some good calls in there," was the first thing my dad said as I walked up to him. I shrugged.

"Jayden would disagree," I muttered. My dad's eyes narrowed. Whenever I looked at him, all I could see was my own face staring back at me. I always wondered if my future face would look like his one day, or if I will age more gracefully like my mom's side of the family.

"Jayden has always been like that," my father said, nodding his head at his words. "He's a really great player—I dare say, he might become better than his own dad—but he has a serious anger problem. It could cut his career short, don't you think?" I shrugged at his words. I didn't know whether his talent would overcome his attitude or not when it came to coaches.

"It's the first time he was ejected from a game," I pointed out, "Ever."

"Ever?" my dad repeated, his normally small, hooded eyes wide. I nodded, sheepishly. My dad let out a low whistle.

"He's going to be pretty upset with you," he said, nonchalantly.

"He *is* upset with me. I mean, he came out of the locker room *just* to glare at me and then walked away!" I exclaimed, annoyed. My dad chuckled.

"That kid has always been a bit petty with you," he said. My dad knew most of the issues that Jayden and I had growing up. He was the person that I would go to in order to complain, rant, and vent about Jayden. Once I started seeing Dr. Adler, I stopped complaining about Jayden as much, but sometimes it would just come out.

"Well," my dad said as we walked over to his car, "His dad was watching today." My head whipped around to look at him in the face. He looked surprised by the action.

"What?"

"His dad was here?" I asked.

"Yes."

"James King was at the game?" I asked again, incredulously. My dad nodded his head.

"No, there's no way," I said, shaking my head, "The announcers would've said something."

"He was there secretly. I only recognized him because, well, for one, he's very tall and for the other, you've been going to school with Jayden since you were young. So he's easily recognizable to me."

"There's just no way," I repeated. My dad stared at me with an eyebrow raised and shook his head. The only thing I could think about was Jayden's words that he said to me before the game: *"This game's really important for me."*

"Ah fuck," I muttered. My dad immediately put a frown on his face.

"Language, Eun-hye," my dad said, calling me by my Korean name. I felt my phone vibrate in my back pocket and looked at the contact.

"Sorry, Appa," I said, using the Korean word for dad, "I have to go."

"Remember to come over for dinner tomorrow! Your brother will be there with your nephew!" my dad said. I gave him a quick hug and then started walking fast towards my hotel. The name "Will" was flashing over my phone as it rang. I quickly answered.

"Are you serious, Grace?" he immediately said.

"Hi to you, too," I muttered.

"I get that it's your birthday but, God," he sighed.

"Did Jayden talk to you?" I asked.

"Barely. I called him, but he barely said two words to me and then hung up. You know his anger extends to me when you do things to him," Will ranted. I rolled my eyes.

"I'm sorry that he does that but that's technically not my fault," I pointed out. *It's his*, I wanted to say but didn't.

"Did you know his dad was at that game?" Will asked. I stayed silent. Will breathed out a loud sigh.

"So you knew."

"Not beforehand I didn't!" I exclaimed. "Besides, I was just doing my job. You can't blame me for just doing my job!" Some passersby looked at me strangely as I tried to avert eye contact. I was almost at my hotel building, *thank God*.

"You know his dad never came to his games growing up," Will said, almost accusingly. Yeah, of course I knew. Jayden had daddy issues. His dad was the only person that could make him shut down for weeks on end. I knew that more than anybody considering *I* was the one officiating some of his games since high school. But, I wasn't going to lecture Will on that.

"This is the first game his dad has been to since Jayden started playing in the NBA," Will continued.

"And the first game he goes to, his son gets kicked out? He probably will never go to another one."

"Honestly, Will," I said, struggling with my hotel key, "How is that my fault?"

"It's not *just* your fault," Will sighed. "I just wish you turned a bit of a blind eye."

"First of all," I said, finally getting into my hotel room, "It's not in my job description to placate basketball players. And second of all, I did try to *kind of* turn a blind eye. But, it's hard when he makes such obvious fouls. If I didn't call it, one of the other refs would've."

"It probably would've been better if another ref did, instead of you," Will muttered.

"What do you mean?" I asked, sitting down on the white, pristine hotel bed.

"I mean, Jayden is out for blood. I've never seen him this angry," Will said. Jayden's dark eyes flashed across my mind.

"Yeah," I mumbled, "Neither have I." Will finished the conversation by wishing me a happy birthday and complaining to me about how his roommate was always bringing over a new girl every week and how annoying it was. We said our good-byes and I immediately flopped down onto the bed. Just as I was starting to relax, I felt my phone vibrate again. Groaning, I rolled over onto my belly and answered it.

"Grace," it was Dr. Adler again. This was the second time that he was calling me today, and that was pretty unusual for him.

"Dr. Adler," I said, mocking his tone of voice a little. He was silent for a moment.

"Sorry," I said, quickly.

"It's fine. I was just worried for a moment. Are you still thinking about Jayden?" he asked. I sighed as I pulled the hair tie from my bun, letting my black hair fall over my bird-like shoulders.

"Yeah. Apparently his dad was at the game, and I didn't know," I said.

"It's not your fault that he got ejected from the game," Dr. Adler said, guessing at how I felt.

"I know, but why does it feel like it is?" I asked.

"How *do* you feel?" he asked.

"I just feel like everything that happens to Jayden is somehow my fault. I know I made the calls and that technically kicked him out of the game. But, isn't what he did the cause for him getting kicked out? He's the one who made those fouls. But, my friend Will just called me to talk about how angry Jayden is. And, like, why should *I* be so concerned about whether Jayden is angry or not? He's unusually upset tonight, and I am afraid that he's going to do something he might regret, but none of that is my fault. Is it?" Dr. Adler was quiet for a minute.

"Well, I've always said you should stop being friends with Will. We should continue this conversation at our session this week. But, I do want to say, it isn't your fault. You can't control how Jayden is feeling. Only Jayden can recognize and control his own impulses, not you," he said. I let out a breath that I had been holding in. A weight felt like it was lifted from my shoulders. I just needed someone to tell me that it wasn't because of me that Jayden was angry, but rather that it was because of himself.

"Have you taken your anxiety medication today?" Dr. Adler asked. I nodded my head as I answered.

"Yeah, I took it this morning."

"Hmm, okay. Maybe take another pill," he said. "I will definitely talk to your psychiatrist about upping the dosage. I think it'll be beneficial for you."

"Thanks for calling me, Dr. Adler," I said.

"Of course," he said. "You can always count on me." As I hung up my cell phone, the hotel phone started to ring.

"God, what is up with everyone calling me today?" I muttered as I picked up the phone.

"Miss Lee?" a voice asked.

"This is she," I answered.

"There's a delivery for you at the front desk."

* * *

The lady at the front desk handed me a gift basket as I looked at her, bewildered. A gift basket? Who was sending me a gift basket?

"Boyfriend?" she asked, a knowing smile on her face. I frowned at her words.

"I don't have one," I said. Her smile slowly disappeared.

"Ah," is all she said and I took that embarrassing

moment as my cue to leave. I lugged the giant gift basket up to my room as I thought about who could send me something like this. As I started to think maybe it was from Will for my birthday, my phone vibrated. I put the basket down on the side table, next to the bed.

Did you get Jayden's thing? He said he sent something, the text from Will read. *Oh,* I thought, so this was Jayden's apology.

How did he get this so late at night? I texted back after opening the plastic wrapping surrounding the basket. Inside were various cookies and a bottle of wine. I looked for a note, some form of written apology, but there was nothing. Of course Jayden wouldn't *actually* apologize.

Who knows? It's Jayden, Will's text read. I stared at the basket for a long while and then shrugged. *Fuck it,* I thought. I might as well drink the wine. I grabbed the bottle and twisted the top open. It was my favorite wine: Roscato. I didn't particularly enjoy alcohol that much. I didn't like how it made me feel, or the hives that would inevitably appear all over my arms and legs. It also didn't help that I turned as red as a tomato and that splotches would appear on my face. I was the ugliest drunk I think the world had ever seen, so I wasn't much for drinking. But today... Today was stressful. I could feel myself start to melt away as I sipped on the wine.

Wait a minute, I sat up straighter as I stared at the basket of sweets. My vision started to blur and a burning sensation became stronger around my lips. As I gasped for air, I stared hard at the plastic wine glass that was starting to fall out of my numb hands. Everything around me started to become sideways, and then I realized I had fallen onto the bed. Pain and confusion erupted in my body as what had happened started to sink in. The spilled wine on the bed was a giant splotch that seemed to create the outline of a small basketball player.

I knew I was dying, but my last thoughts were only: *How did Jayden know Roscato was my favorite wine?*

five

WHEN I WOKE UP, it felt like hours had passed. I glanced over at the clock and, to my surprise, I was only out of it for ten minutes. *That was some weird wine,* I thought to myself as I started to get up. I held my pounding head in my hands and then felt my heart stop. Or, felt... what would've been my heart stopping. Except, as it turned out, I didn't have a heart anymore. Or... life anymore, for that matter.

Sprawled out across the bed was my lifeless corpse. Gray film had started to encase my usually bright, brown eyes and they just stared out into noth-ingness. *Nothingness.* I stared in shock.

I was dead.

Me, Grace Lee. I had died.

I was... murdered?

Was I murdered?

Why was there only blackness after I died?

Wait, why am I still alive?

Or... oh my God, am I a *ghost?*

A million thoughts raced through my... phantom brain, I guess. I didn't understand what had happened to me. I looked down at my ghostly figure, and it didn't look like I was dead. At least to me. In movies, the ghosts always were a little see-through, but I definitely did not look see-through. And I didn't think I *could* be see-through since I was still sitting on the bed. However, when I went to text Will that I was dead, my hand wasn't able to touch the phone.

"I thought ghosts could manipulate technology," I muttered to myself. My eyes wandered back over to the spilled wine on the bed. I couldn't believe that Jayden would poison me. And just as I thought this, the world around me blurred as if I were moving incredibly fast. Before I could even blink, I was standing in front of Jayden and a girl on the dance team making out.

"Oh my *God!*" I exclaimed as I turned around quickly. The only thing I could register before turning quickly around was that Jayden definitely had his shirt off and that's all I needed to know.

"Grace?" I heard him say. I stayed turned around as I heard him get up and throw on a T-shirt.

"You can see me?" I felt myself ask.

"Who are you talking to?" the girl next to him said. I turned around slightly to look at a bewildered Jayden.

"*What* are you doing in my apartment? No—*how* did you even get *in?*" he asked. He locked his jaw a little bit, which is what he did when he was annoyed.

"How did I get in? That's rich, coming from you," I gave a dry laugh. It was all I could do to start breaking down. I was dead. And... *obviously* I was murdered. By none other than Jayden himself.

"Seriously, Jay, you're freaking me out," the girl said, her face contorted into concern as she stared up at Jayden. Luckily, she was fully clothed.

"What? How am *I* freaking you out?" Jayden asked, tearing his eyes away from me in order to give the girl the same annoyed face that he was just giving me.

"Who are you talking to?" she asked, her voice a little smaller.

"What do you mean 'who am I talking to?' She's literally standing right in front of you," Jayden said, gesturing over at me. I felt myself laugh, but it had a bit of a different ring to it. It sounded slightly bitter.

"She can't see me," I said, almost matter-of-factly.

"What are you guys even talking about, bro," Jayden said, sitting back down on his couch. He put his hands up in frustration and stared at me, hard.

"There's no one in front of us, Jay," the girl whispered, after a moment. Jayden stared at her like she was crazy.

"You seriously can't see this crazy Asian girl standing in front of us?" he asked. She stared right at me, but I could tell that her eyes saw through me. To her, I really wasn't there.

"I'm dead, Jayden," I said. My voice sounded

slightly far away and I could feel myself about to cry. His head whipped over to look at me. His eyes were always so large on his face, almost comically, but just now they seemed to take up his entire expression.

"What the fuck are you talking about, Grace?" I could tell that he was starting to get pissed off. The girl stared at Jayden for a little longer and then grabbed her purse that was sitting next to her.

"I think I'm just gonna go," she muttered. Jayden grabbed her arm as she walked past.

"You seriously don't see her?" he asked, his eyes searching hers for any hint of a joke. She carefully pulled her arm away and tried to smile at him.

"You've had a long day, I get it. Terrible night. I'll hit you up tomorrow," she said, walking towards the door. I knew she was not going to hit him up tomorrow, and the thought almost made me euphoric. Jayden stared at her as she exited his apartment, and his head moved back towards me like a zombie.

"Grace, you better start to explain this shit to me. Like right now," he demanded.

"I already told you," I said, my voice getting louder. "I'm *fucking* dead." Jayden's eyebrows raised at my sudden cursing. I wasn't one to curse normally, but I was *freaking out.*

"Okay, how can you be dead if you're standing right in front of me?" Jayden asked, his voice annoyingly calm.

"Oh, let me think," I said, putting my hand to my

chin as I pretended to think. "Oh right. Maybe it's because you fucking *poisoned* my wine?"

"What wine?" Jayden exploded.

"The wine that you sent me in that stupid apology basket of cookies!" I yelled.

"*What* basket of cookies??? What are you saying to me, Grace, for real?" Jayden stood up, getting out of his couch, as he got closer to me. I hated that I had to stare up at him during this confrontation.

"Are you telling me that you didn't send that basket of cookies with a bottle of Roscato wine?" I asked. He stared at me like I was crazy.

"No offense, Grace—since I know it's your birthday and everything—but like, why the fuck would *I* send *you* a basket of fucking *cookies*?" he asked. I paused for a moment. He *did* have a point. It was pretty out of character for him.

"Because you were pretty mean to me during the game and obviously wanted to send an apology about your behavior," I said, but even as I was saying this it sounded plain ridiculous to me. He stared at me, incredulously.

"If anyone was mean to anybody, it would be you being mean to me," he said. I rolled my eyes.

"I was just doing my job," I said. "You were the one who wasn't doing yours. It's not my fault that—" He put a giant hand up, blocking my view.

"I don't want to hear your annoying voice anymore," he said, moving his hand. I stared up at him in disbelief.

"If you didn't send me that basket of cookies, then who did?" I asked. He shrugged as he moved back to sit on the couch.

"Beats me," he said, flopping down onto the couch. He grabbed the TV remote and started watching reruns of reality TV shows that sometimes would come on. I stood in front of him, blocking his view of the TV. He glared at me.

"Will texted me saying that you sent me something. I know you killed me, don't lie," I said, trying to corner him into admitting his crime. His face scrunched together in distaste.

"Yeah, I sent you something. But, it wasn't a basket of cookies and wine. It was a smashed up birthday cake with a note telling you to go fuck yourself," he said this so casually that it almost sounded like a normal action that someone would do.

"Right, of course," I muttered.

"I wouldn't fucking poison you," he pointed out. "That's psychotic."

"And a smashed birthday cake telling me to go fuck myself isn't?" I asked. This man was insane. He almost giggled to himself at the thought.

"It *was* a pretty funny thing to do," he pointed out.

"You bought a birthday cake—"

"It had your name on it and everything," he laughed.

"—And then smashed it and sent it to me and you don't think that you're absolutely insane?" I finished my thought.

"I didn't poison you, though," he said. He then stared at me, as if he were looking for something in my face or body.

"You don't *look* dead," he finally said after surveying me. I glared at him as I gestured to my body.

"I am *obviously* dead. How else did I get here?" I seethed.

"Will could've given you the code to my apartment. And I can see you sneaking in here to watch me make out with Allison," he said, crossing his arms over his chest as if he had me all figured out. I stared at him in disgust.

"Why would I want to watch you make out with Allison?" I asked, rhetorically.

"Because you're a—"

"It was a rhetorical question, Jayden. *No one* would want to watch you make out with anyone. You look like a fucking fish when you kiss someone," I said, not letting him finish his sentence.

"So, you were watching." He smirked at me. I hated him. I absolutely hated the hell out of him. Pivoting on the heel of my foot, I started walking towards his apartment door.

"Never mind. I don't even know why I'm here," I muttered.

"See you later, ref," Jayden called out as he started to flip through channels. I rolled my eyes and opened the door. Maybe I wasn't dead. Maybe this was just some weird, uncomfortable nightmare. I thought this as I stepped through the door, only to suddenly wind up back in front of Jayden. I stared down at myself in bewilderment as Jayden's eyes widened, comically.

Sighing, I said, "See? I'm dead."

"Wha-a-a-t the fu-u-uck," Jayden said, prolonging the words. He and I stared at each other for a long while.

"You're dead."

"I know," I said.

"Dude, you're fucking *dead*," Jayden said, getting up to walk around me.

"I *know*," I repeated.

"Why can't you leave me though?" he asked. He stared at me for a moment and then a knowing, toe-curling smile appeared on his lips.

"Is it because you were secretly in—"

"Obviously it's because you killed me," I said, not letting him finish that thought. To hear it out loud, I would *have* to throw up. Except, I wouldn't be able to throw up as I was now a ghost and ghosts didn't have a digestive system... Did they?

"Grace, you don't seriously think that I would've killed you, do you?" he said, leaning back as his head angled down to look at me. My neck was starting to hurt trying to look him in the eyes.

"You're the only person in the world who would try to kill me. Especially after tonight," I pointed out. His brown eyes stared daggers into mine.

"So you knew, huh?" he said, circling back to the couch.

"Well, I didn't know ahead of time. I only knew after my dad told me," I explained.

"Whatever," he said.

"Are you seriously going to stay being mad at me when I'm *dead*?" I asked. He shrugged noncommittally.

"Dunno," he said. "Besides, I don't really believe you're actually dead. There's literally no way because ghosts aren't real. You either go to heaven or hell." I stared at him, incredulously. He put his hands up defensively.

"Hey, I don't make the rules," he said.

"Do you *want* to go see my dead body?" I asked. "Will that be enough to convince you that you killed me?" He stared at me some more.

"I'm just in some weird nightmare, aren't I?" he asked. *You and me both*, I thought.

"I wish," I muttered instead. He pushed himself off of the couch, stretched, and then smirked at me.

"Okay, I can see that you're still going to play this game with me. If you want me to see your 'dead body,'" he put his fingers up to do air quotes, "then I'll go along with you."

"You're going to be incredibly shocked," I warned.

"Oh-kay," he said, in a voice that surely didn't believe me. I smiled to myself. Jayden King was about to be in for a big surprise.

six

JAYDEN STARED at my sprawled out body with his eyes wide from shock. His jaw was opened slightly, and he couldn't take his eyes off of my dead corpse that was laid out on the bed. Even I had to admit, it was a morbid sight. That body barely looked like me without life animating it.

The hotel worker that let us into the room ran out, face white as a ghost, saying that he was going to call 911. Once the worker was far enough down the hallway, Jayden grabbed the small trash can that was in the room and emptied whatever he ate into it. I turned away in disgust.

"Are you done?" I asked, once the sound of bile hitting tin was silenced.

"I'm looking at your dead body," he said, his voice sounding hollow and hoarse. The sound of his voice elicited an emotional response in my ghostly body. I fought the urge to start crying.

"Yeah," I simply said.

"You really think I would do something like this to you?" he asked, his eyes desperately searching mine. What they were looking for, I didn't know. I shrugged.

"I don't know," I muttered.

"I have to call Will," Jayden said, his voice sounding far away. There was barely any life in it.

"You know, maybe we should go," I said.

"Why?" Jayden asked. I stared at the wine that was spilled on the bed. It was pale pink now, the comforter having soaked up most of the liquid. But, it still was in the weird shape of a basketball player about to make a dunk.

"I just think it's bad that you're here," I said. "I *was* murdered."

"You think the cops will think *I* did this?" he asked. I shrugged with one shoulder.

"Who knows?" I said. "*I* thought that you did." Jayden stared at me for a moment and then looked at my corpse again.

"If I leave, I look more suspicious," he said, barely above a whisper. I stared at him, a bit of pity tugging at my heart. I felt bad, bringing him here. Especially considering he didn't really like the cops, for good reason.

"I'm sorry," I said.

"For dying?" he asked, smiling a little.

"For bringing you here," I said, honestly. He shrugged.

"It'll be in the news, for sure," he muttered. "But,

it's fine. I'm the one who didn't believe you were a ghost..." His voice trailed off as his eyes widened.

"Do you think I'm tripping?" he asked. I shrugged.

"I feel pretty real to me," I assured.

"You would say that, if I was crazy," he breathed.

"You can't say that you see the ghost of me to the cops," I pointed out. He stared at me like I was the one seeing a ghost.

"Why would I *tell* them that? I may be tripping right now, Grace, but I ain't stupid," he retorted. My eyebrows raised as I shrugged my shoulders.

"Could've fooled me," I said. Hearing some commotion down the hallway, I peered out the open door to see EMTs and police officers coming quickly towards my room.

"You better start looking sad," I said. "They're coming."

"I *am* sad, G," he barely muttered. But, he quickly put on a sad face.

"Yeah," I scoffed, "You definitely look it." He quickly glared at me as the emergency personnel started coming in. A cop stood at the entrance of the room and stared at Jayden as he tried to just look as sad as he could.

"Sadder," I said. He glanced at me as if he were saying: *How can I possibly look any sadder?* The cop leaned forward slightly to get a good look at Jayden's face.

"Oh, you're that one basketball player, aren't you?"

the cop said, snapping his fingers as he tried to think of Jayden's name. Jayden nodded.

"You play for the Washington Wolves, right?" he asked, taking his phone out of his back pocket.

"Yeah, I do. I'm Jayden King," Jayden said, putting a hand to his chest.

"Jayden King—James King's son! Oh, man, your dad is a legend," the cop said, his eyes lighting up excitedly.

"Yup," Jayden quietly responded, nodding his head.

"Do you think I could get a picture with you real quick?" the cop asked. Jayden stared at him for a long while.

"Man, my friend just died," Jayden said, gesturing towards my corpse. The cop glanced over at my dead body and nodded his head.

"Oh, right," the cop said, staring at my dead body that was being photographed by forensics. There was a long silence and then the cop turned towards Jayden, with his phone still in his hand.

"Just real quick? I'm a huge fan," the cop said. Jayden's eyes narrowed.

"You didn't even remember my—You know what? Sure, whatever," Jayden said, deciding not to argue with the police. He rubbed his eyes and then grimaced —though he tried to smile—for the picture. The cop smiled brilliantly next to Jayden and snapped the photo. He looked at the selfie, smiling to himself, and then turned off his phone.

"We're going to need to question you though, back at the station," the cop said. Jayden stared at me, annoyed with the cop.

"Yeah, for sure. No problem, man," Jayden muttered. He widened his eyes and gave me a look of: *Can you believe this guy?* I laughed.

"He's obviously a *huge* fan," I said.

"Couldn't even remember my name and asked for a photo at a crime scene," Jayden barely whispered.

"Sorry, son? I didn't quite catch that," the cop said. Jayden's face went back into sad mode and he turned towards the cop.

"I was just saying some prayers for my friend," Jayden lied. The cop gestured for Jayden to follow him outside of the hotel room.

"So, we're going to need to take your testimony, just so we understand what happened here," the cop said. His partner then came up and looked over at Jayden.

"Are you Jayden King? The basketball player?" the cop's partner said. He had a giant mustache and it was the only thing I could stare at.

"Yup, that's me," Jayden muttered.

"We can't let this guy go to the station," Giant Mustache said to his partner. "It'll be crowded with paparazzi, if they get word about him being here."

"Okay, son, we'll take your testimony here then," the cop said, pulling out a notepad.

"Sure, that works for me," Jayden said as people

started taping up the entrance to my hotel room with yellow tape that read "CRIME SCENE DO NOT CROSS" over and over on it. The EMTs had started rolling my dead body down the hallway towards the exit. Seeing it made me feel dizzy, and even Jayden looked a bit paler.

"So, how do you know the victim?" the cop asked.

"Uh, I've known Grace Lee since sixth grade. We went to school together and she's also a ref in the league," Jayden answered, focusing his gaze on the cop.

"What were you doing, visiting her hotel room?" his steel blue eyes stared at Jayden. It was as if all the small talk from earlier never happened.

"Tell him that you came because I didn't respond to your prank. They're going to find out about that so you might as well talk about it now," I said. Jayden glanced at me, made a face as he thought about what I said, and then nodded slightly.

"Well, I don't know if you watched tonight's game, but she was the ref tonight and I got kicked out. She and I have known each other for a while. It was her birthday today, and I played a prank on her. Our relationship is kind of... I tease her and she yells at me. You know, that kind of thing," Jayden explained. The cop nodded his head as he wrote down what Jayden was saying.

"Relationship?" I barely coughed out. Jayden gave me a pleading glance mixed with a glare.

"And what kind of prank was it?" the cop asked. Jayden rubbed the back of his head as he laughed a little.

"I ki-i-inda sent her a smashed birthday cake with a note that said for her to... go fuck herself," Jayden let out a little laugh at the end of his explanation. The cop's eyebrows raised as he wrote down what he said.

"You're making yourself look *so* bad right now," I laughed. Jayden tried hard not to glare at me for a moment.

"Okay... And you were here, why?" the cop asked.

"Usually, she reacts by calling and yelling at me. She didn't this time, so I went to go see her reaction in person," Jayden said.

"And when you got here—"

"She was dead," Jayden said, quietly. His eyes did look incredibly sad, I had to admit. The cop closed the notepad that he was holding with the flick of his wrist.

"Okay, Mr. King, that should be all for now. If we have any more questions, we'll contact you," the cop said. Jayden nodded and handed him a business card from his sweatpants.

"Call me if you need any more information," Jayden said. The cop nodded and took the card, giving Jayden a swift handshake in the process.

"It was good meeting you," the cop said.

"Do you think I could get a picture with ya?" Giant Mustache asked, stepping out of the room.

"Seriously?" Jayden muttered. Giant Mustache leaned forward and raised an eyebrow.

"Sorry, I didn't catch that," Giant Mustache said.

"I said sure," Jayden responded, smiling. But, his smile didn't quite reach his eyes.

"DAMN, I GOTTA CALL WILL," Jayden muttered, again, his hands in his pockets as we walked down the streets of D.C. back to his apartment.

"Can you call my dad?" I asked, quietly. Jayden looked at me incredulously.

"G, how am I gonna call your dad? I barely know the guy and suddenly I got his phone number? You got me fucked up," he said.

"You think it'll make you look suspicious?" I asked, meekly.

"*Yeah*, I think it'll make me look suspicious," he said, nodding his head. "Will can call your dad."

"Fine, I guess call Will," I said. Jayden took out his cell phone and scrolled until he saw Will's name. He pressed the call button. Jayden walked faster, putting his hood up, as the phone rang.

"Will?" Jayden said. His brown eyes glanced over

at me and he laughed slightly. "You're not going to believe what happened."

"What?" I heard Will ask on the other line. "Is Grace mad at you again?"

"Grace is dead," Jayden said, his voice cracking a bit on the "dead" part.

"Aw, you *do* care," I said. He squinted at me.

"She's dead and now she's haunting me," he said.

After a long silence, Will finally said, "*What?*"

"I said that Grace is dead and now she's haunting me," Jayden said a little louder. I rolled my eyes.

"He wasn't asking you to repeat yourself, you dumbass," I said as I heard Will say over the phone, "I didn't want you to repeat yourself, you idiot." I smiled to myself. Will and I still were in sync, even in death.

"Okay, okay, I got it. I don't know how you and Grace say the same things sometimes," Jayden muttered.

"Are you sure that you're not, like, terribly drunk because it is, like... four in the morning," Will said.

"I'm not drunk. She's dead," Jayden said, whispering the last part. He stared at me for a moment and then said: "You know what? We're gonna come over."

"Who's we?"

"Grace's ghost and I," Jayden said, and then he hung up the phone.

* * *

Will stared at me, though it was clear that he saw through me and was only seeing an empty space. Jayden kept gesturing towards me, as if that would make Will see me more.

"Please tell me you see her," Jayden finally said, filling the silence.

"I don't see anything," Will said, quietly. He pulled the blue robe that he had owned since he was thirteen —also the age where he stopped growing—tighter around his waist.

"Why can't he see you?" Jayden asked me. I shrugged.

"I don't know. Why can *you* see me? *If* you didn't kill me," I pointed out. Jayden gave me an incredulous look.

"For the last time, G, I seriously did not kill you," he hissed. Will's barely there eyebrows were raised as he watched this conversation between what he saw was Jayden and the air.

"Jayden... have you started doing drugs?" Will asked slowly. Jayden's head turned to look at Will.

"You know I would never do drugs," Jayden said, pointing at Will. That was a surprise to hear. I always thought Jayden would be someone who would do drugs, or at least try them. They stared each other down for a moment.

"Okay, tell Will that you'll tell him something that only I would know," I said, wanting to help the situation. Jayden nodded at me and then crossed his arms as he looked down at Will.

"Grace says she'll tell you something that only she would know, so that way you know that she's a ghost and that she's haunting me," Jayden said. An eyebrow raised on Will's freckled face.

"Proceed," he said.

"Tell him that he peed in his drawer when he was six while he was half asleep during a sleepover and that it was traumatizing for me," I said. Jayden stared at me, stunned.

"That really happened?" he asked.

"Yup," I said, tightening my lips into a thin line as I nodded my head. Worst sleepover ever, and it was the last. I never slept over at Will's house again after that. Jayden breathed out.

"Okay," he said, turning towards Will, "So-o-o, Grace says that during a sleepover when you guys were six..." Will stared in horror at Jayden.

"When did she tell you this?" Will asked, taking a step forward. "She swore to secrecy. To her grave."

"I *am* at my grave, basically," I muttered.

"Grace literally just told me. That's how I know!" Jayden explained.

"Tell him that you know that he and his one and only girlfriend broke up because after she kissed him, he threw up in her mouth," I said.

"No, bro, that really happened?" Jayden asked, shocked and a bit disappointed. He shook his head as he turned back towards Will.

"What did she say?" Will asked, his foot tapping from nerves.

"You didn't tell me that's why you and Shyla broke up," Jayden said, quietly. Will looked at where he thought I was in horror.

"She's really there," Will whispered.

"I know," Jayden whispered back, staring at me.

"When did she die? I just texted her a few hours ago," Will muttered, sitting down on his couch. His hands gripped the armrest, knuckles white at the morbid news. Jayden sat down next to him as I sat down on the armchair. It didn't move as I sat down, like it normally would've. I was weightless.

"I guess a few hours ago, then," Jayden shrugged. "She just appeared at my apartment and started accusing me of killing her."

"Which you most likely did," I mumbled.

"I didn't kill you, G, I swear," Jayden said, exasperated. Will looked over at the armchair and then back at Jayden.

"You really look like a crazy person when you're talking to her," Will pointed out.

"I know," Jayden said, dejected.

"Why does she think you killed her?" Will asked.

"Because who else would poison me?" I exclaimed.

"She thinks someone poisoned her," Jayden sighed as he leaned back into the couch.

"And the likely culprit *would* be you," Will finished, putting a hand to his chin.

"See!" I said, gesturing towards Will, "I'm not the only one who thinks you would kill me." Jayden ignored me as he stared straight ahead.

"So, she appeared to you and then you went and saw her body?" Will asked. Jayden nodded his head.

"I thought she was playing some kind of prank on me. I didn't think she'd actually be dead," Jayden sighed.

"You think she's haunting you?" Will asked.

"I mean," Jayden gestured towards me, "What would you call this? *You* can't see her and you were her best friend." Will nodded his head. He turned towards me, and I could tell that he felt silly looking at the empty armchair and trying to imagine his best friend was sitting in it.

"It's really unfair of you to not let me see you as a ghost, Grace. After all we've been through," Will chastised as he shook his head.

"I'm sorry, Will. It wasn't my decision," I said.

"She says she's sorry and she didn't make it like that," Jayden quickly said for me. I couldn't help but think that wasn't what I said *but whatever.*

"It is weird that only you can see her as a ghost, especially since the connection is that you didn't kill her," Will mused.

"Thank you! Please tell her that I'm not capable of murder," Jayden exclaimed.

"He wouldn't have poisoned you, Grace. He never hated you that much," Will muttered in my direction. Did he not? That was hard to believe. I rolled my eyes.

"What were you thinking about when you died?" Will asked, his eyes staring past me. It was unnerving, noticing that his eyes couldn't focus on my body or my face.

"I was thinking about..." I let myself drift off as my eyes widened. I was thinking about Jayden. I couldn't let Jayden know that my last thoughts when I was alive were about him.

"Wine," I finished. A knowing eyebrow raised on Jayden's face.

"She was obviously thinking about me," he said to Will. Will nodded his head in agreement.

"Can you please—I was *not* thinking about you! Can you tell him what I said, not what you think?" I stammered.

"Okay," Jayden held up a hand in order to stop my panicked words, "She *says* that she was thinking about wine, but she paused for a weird amount of time, her eyes widened, and then she said it was wine. So obviously it was me, right? That's why she's haunting me?" I didn't know Jayden was so perceptive with my facial expressions. Or rather, I didn't know I was so expressive, as I must've been because otherwise, how would he notice me widening my eyes for a split second?

"It sounds like she was thinking about you, yes," Will agreed.

"I was not thinking about you, Jayden. Why would I be thinking about you?" I fumed.

"Maybe because you thought I poisoned the wine. Would there be a different reason, perhaps?" Jayden teased. I stared at him for a long while. He had a point. I could've just said that in the first place. Well, I *did* think he poisoned the wine and that's *why* I was thinking about him. I shook my head.

"I don't really remember what I was thinking about. I just remember it was about the wine," I mumbled. Jayden clapped his hands together.

"Okay, so she admitted she was thinking about me —" I started to protest but he continued, "—in regards to the wine."

"So because she was thinking that you poisoned the wine, you're the only one who can see her," Will explained. "I feel like that makes sense."

"How do I get rid of her?" Jayden asked.

"Why are you asking me?" Will retorted.

"You're smart. I feel like you would know," Jayden responded. Will twisted his lips as he thought.

"She can't just leave?" he asked.

"When she tries to leave, she just appears right back in front of me," Jayden explained. Will glanced over in my direction.

"Let's try it again," he said. I sighed and got up. I wished I could leave Jayden's presence, that would be amazing. I hoped after finding out that he didn't poison the wine, it'll turn out that I can haunt the person who did. And then maybe move on into nothingness, or whatever came after death. I walked through the door of Will's apartment to only see a blur of colors and appear right in front of Jayden again. Jayden gave out a shout of surprise as I appeared right in front of his feet.

"Don't do that," he demanded as he collected himself.

"I didn't do it on purpose," I grumbled, making my way back to the armchair. Will stared at Jayden and pursed his lips.

"So she wasn't able to leave," Will said, stroking his chin. He did this all the time when he thought, despite not having a beard.

"She was poisoned by wine that was given to her by somebody. Grace thought it was you, but it wasn't. And now she's not able to leave," Will said, slowly. I nodded along with his thoughts, until I came to the realization that I knew Will was coming to. *No*, I thought, *I hope that it's not that I have to—*

"You have to help her find her murderer," Will finished my thought. *Fuuuuu—*

eight

AND THAT'S how I ended up at my own funeral a week later with Jayden taking notes on everyone I used to know. The funeral was really just a memorial service, though, as my body was still going through an autopsy. Outside of the church were a bunch of photographers, having already heard how the legendary basketball player's son was the one who found me dead. It was kind of disrespectful, them showing up to my funeral just to get pictures of Jayden mourning his "friend."

"How well did you know that girl?" Jayden whispered, pointing his pen in the direction of my cousin.

"She's my cousin," I said, adding, "From Korea."

"So couldn't have been her, then," Jayden mused as he crossed out the words "Girl with straight black hair wearing black clothes." I scoffed at his notes.

"Jayden, that describes most of my family right

now," I pointed. He glared at me and closed his notepad, quickly.

"You weren't supposed to see that," he muttered. I looked around. I watched as Valentina glanced over at Jayden, her eyes knowingly watching him. *She must've known I knew him more than I let on*, I thought. My eyes continued to look at the people in the room. It was weird seeing my family and all the people that I had met in my life cry over my death. The whole ordeal made it feel more... final. During it, my brother talked a bit about how much he loved me and the memories that we shared growing up.

"Now I've lost the two most important women in my life," he ended his speech. Tears welled up in my eyes, and I had to look away. My older brother Joseph never shed a tear when our mom died. To think that he was suffering in agony, for my or my dad's sake, killed me. And to have him go through losing his sister... I looked away.

"Are you okay?" Jayden whispered, staring at me. I shook my head.

"I'm fine," I muttered my mantra. The only two words that have gotten me through life.

"Sorry," Jayden barely breathed, "I have to be here." He was right. It's not like he couldn't show up, that would look strange.

"I'm fine," I repeated. He gave me a look that showed he didn't necessarily believe me, and then looked away. No one should have to go through watching one's own funeral. It was a form of torture, and I wondered what I had done in my life to deserve this.

Once the service was over, I saw my dad make eye contact with Jayden and start to walk over. His eyes were swollen, as if he had been crying for days. I had only seen my father cry once, after my mother died. He thought he was alone, but his bedroom door was opened slightly, and I was still able to peer in. I remember how he was on the floor, gripping my mother's pajama shirt, hoping that he could still breathe in her scent.

"You found her that night, right?" my dad asked Jayden. He smoothed down his suit jacket that didn't quite fit right as he stared intensely up at him. Jayden cleared his throat and nodded.

"Yeah, I found her in her hotel room," he said.

"I'm sorry you had to see her like that," my dad said, putting a hand on Jayden's arm, as he couldn't quite reach his shoulder.

"It's okay. I'm glad I found her," Jayden said, slowly. And then quickly adding, "Not that I'm glad she was dead, but I'd rather it be me than you or Joseph." My dad nodded his head.

"The cops believe it could be... foul play," he said, his words stuck in his throat slightly. I stared at him, wondering what my father was thinking. How horrible it must be to hear that your daughter was potentially murdered.

"I think it was too," Jayden said, confidently. "It looked like the wine she drank was what killed her."

"The police told me that as well. The autopsy isn't done yet, though," my dad whispered. He put a hand to his nose as he pinched the bridge.

"I promised her mother I'd protect her," my father whispered. "Mi-an-hae, oori ddal." *I'm sorry, my daughter.* He barely breathed those Korean words, but I could hear them still. My ears felt wet, as if the tears of my father had fallen on them as the words drifted into my brain.

"Appa," I whispered, tears welling up in my eyes.

"You did everything that you could," Jayden consoled, though he looked incredibly uncomfortable with the conversation. I tried to not notice his eyes glancing over at me before turning back to my father to say, "This isn't your fault."

"I was with her that night," my dad said. "I should've stayed with her."

"Everyone always has regrets," Jayden said. "But you had no way of knowing. It's not your fault." I really appreciated Jayden comforting my dad at this moment. For a second, he looked kind and... thoughtful. But, if he thought I was going to thank him for this, he was sorely mistaken.

He was never sympathetic towards me, even after my mother died. A day after she died, I still went to school to take an exam. And he said to me, when the exam results came back a week later, "Your mom is probably super pissed about your grade right now. Rolling around in her grave and everything." Like, *why* would anyone say that?

"Grace was always harsh to you," my dad said after a while, "But, I think you made her life interesting. She seemed to always have a lot of fun with you." Jayden stared at my father, for what seemed like a very long time, and then nodded his head after I scoffed. I had a lot of fun with *him*? My dad must've been delusional from grief.

They stood like that, for a moment, just watching as people left the church. Eventually, my father left and Jayden took that as his cue to leave. He slipped through the back doors of the church, trying to avoid getting photographed. Will pulled up in his beat up minivan that used to be his mother's and gestured for Jayden to come in. I went through the sliding back doors without opening them, settling myself into the backseat.

"That was incredibly depressing," Jayden muttered.

"It was a funeral," Will pointed out. "For our friend."

"Was Grace ever *really* my friend?" Jayden asked, though it sounded like he was asking himself.

"I'm literally sitting right here," I said. He turned his head to look at me sitting in the backseat, sighed dramatically, and then turned around.

"I can't even properly mourn for her because, to

me, it's like she's still alive," Jayden said, pulling at his tie.

"Yeah, I can't imagine being able to see and hear her still," Will said, sarcastically. "I'm sure it's the worst torture ever."

"Bro, I'd trade places with you *any* day," Jayden muttered.

"Do you have any idea who might've murdered her?" Will asked. Jayden shook his head.

"I'm not a detective. I have no idea. Everyone there looked like they were really super sad about her dying," Jayden said.

"Oh, and you're not super sad?" I asked, leaning forward in my seat. Jayden looked around, as if he couldn't see me.

"It's like I can still hear her," he said, feigning sadness.

"Shut up," I muttered.

"Is there really no one who you thought hated you?" Will asked, talking to me even though he couldn't see me.

"No one besides Jayden," I said.

"She said no one," Jayden said. I glared at him.

"You really need to stop summarizing what I'm saying," I warned.

"Or what?"

"Or else," I said.

"*Ooo*, I'm so scared," Jayden said, waving his hands in front of my face. He leaned back into his seat again.

"You're already haunting me. It can't get worse than this."

"It *could* get worse," I said. "I could make sure you look crazy to every single person for the rest of your life."

"We need to find out who murdered her, as soon as possible," Jayden said to Will. "I can't deal with her."

"We'll just need to go through every single person who was in your life, Grace," Will said. "I think that will be the only way to figure it out."

* * *

I had been watching Jayden flip through TV channels in his apartment for the past three hours. Any time that there was something that I might've wanted to watch, he would immediately change the channel and disregard my protests. This was hell. I was sure of it.

"Don't you have practice or a game or something?" I asked. He shrugged his shoulders.

"I'm taking a day off," he muttered. "My supposed 'friend' just died, you know. So, I have to act like I'm mourning."

"Are you *not* in mourning?" I asked, crossing my arms. Jayden rolled his eyes.

"Please," Jayden said, his voice monotone, "Just leave me alone."

"I wish I could, Jayden. I really wish I could," I mumbled under my breath. Honestly, what did I do in my life to deserve this? Why was I attached to Jayden, of all people?

Jayden stuffed a handful of chips into his mouth as I scrunched my nose up in disgust. Without looking at me, he shook a hand that held a chip in my face.

"You know," he started, eating the chip, "There were probably a ton of people who hated you enough to kill you." I stared at him in disbelief.

"Why would you say that to me?" I barely said.

"I'm just saying, G. There's gotta be someone that you know that you've wronged in some way," he pointed out. Someone I've wronged? I never thought that this might've been a revenge killing from anyone other than Jayden.

"I would... have to think about it," I said, slowly.

"What about Shyla? Will's first girlfriend. *She* probably hated you," Jayden mused. My eyebrows scrunched together.

"Why would she hate me?" I asked.

"Well, because you were Will's best friend and a girl," Jayden shrugged, acting like he didn't care about the answer. But, his glance towards me said something different.

"That's not enough of a reason to kill me."

"Okay, well, what about Allen?" he asked, giving me a meaningful stare. I frowned at the thought of Allen, a basketball player that we went to high school with. Last I heard, he was prematurely balding. As he should.

"I don't think Allen has the balls to kill me," I muttered. "Besides, I've never done anything to him." Although, he *did* stop talking to me after junior year. He wouldn't even look at me. Jayden nodded, as if I answered some kind of silent question he was asking.

"There has to be *someone* that you wronged, G. Maybe an ex-boyfriend or something," Jayden sighed. I never dated anyone, but I wasn't about to tell Jayden that. *Who have I wronged?* I mean, I barely talked to anyone besides Will and Jayden and... Valentina. I didn't know Valentina all that well, to be honest. But, have I ever wronged her? I tried to think hard about every interaction that I had with her. Feeling Jayden's stare on me, I relaxed my face so he couldn't see what was on my mind.

"You have someone in mind, don't you?" he said, pointing a long finger at me.

"I don't."

"You do," he said, nodding his head as he leaned back.

"She wouldn't have killed me. I never did anything to her," I protested.

"Why would she be on your mind then?" he asked, pointedly.

"Because—" I paused for a moment. The only reason I had for thinking about her was because I would speak to her fairly often and because I had only just become friends with her. She was almost a stranger.

"I just think she might have some information,

maybe," I mumbled. "She's the only other person I would talk to fairly regularly besides Will and—against my own will—you." Jayden thought for a moment as he looked up at the ceiling.

"You're thinking about Valentina," he said.

nine

JAYDEN TAPPED his veiny fingers on the hotel lobby desk, adjusting his hood, as we waited for Valentina. She had stayed in the area for my funeral, but wasn't available to talk until the day after. The hotel worker put down the phone.

"She'll be down in a moment, Mr. King. If you could wait..." he gestured towards the seating in the lobby. It was a different hotel than the one I died in. A bit more fancier, actually.

"I really don't think she would've killed me," I said, regretting telling Jayden anything. Jayden sat down in a giant chair and his eyes glanced over at me. He put his hand to his mouth so no one would see that he was talking to the air. Though, him putting his hand to his mouth seemed like it would draw more attention, in my opinion.

"She wouldn't have come into your mind if there wasn't a part of you that thought so," he whispered.

"Maybe it's my internalized misogyny coming out," I worried. He made a face.

"What?" he said, then he looked away. The conversation was over. That's one thing that I hated about Jayden. He was always deciding when I could or couldn't talk. He would just make a face, look away, and that was that. I puffed out my cheeks and then started to walk in front of him to continue the conversation, but at that moment, the elevator doors opened. Looking up, I watched as Valentina walked through the doors and she looked... pretty.

"Does she always look this good off court?" Jayden breathed as his eyes took in the sight. She was wearing a baby doll pink dress and her hair was down in bouncy, brown curls. It was... very opposite of her usual style.

"I mean, she's always pretty, but she usually dresses..." *How could I put it?* "More... badass."

"Well, you know me. I love girly girls," he muttered. I narrowed my eyes at him as I thought. He did seem to date girls who were very... cutesy. I subconsciously looked at the outfit that I died in. I was wearing black leggings and an old sweater. Definitely not a "cutesy" style. Then another thought crossed my mind, quickly: *Does Valentina like him?*

"Hi Jayden," Valentina said, once she got close enough. "Do you want to go get some coffee or something?"

"Uh," Jayden looked around, pulling his hood over his head so that no one would recognize him.

Although, anyone would look at a six foot eight Black man wearing a hooded sweatshirt. That wasn't something that people just pretended to not notice.

"This hotel has a courtyard, too, if you want. It's a little bit more private," she offered. Jayden nodded, almost shyly. What was happening in front of my eyes right now? I tried hard not to gag.

Jayden followed Valentina through the hotel as they walked towards the courtyard. They walked almost side by side, with Valentina slightly in front. I watched them from behind. Valentina didn't know that I knew Jayden, before I died. Due to the rules of the league, I had to hide the fact that I knew him, even though we weren't even remotely friends. But, that meant that I couldn't even tell Valentina for fear that I would be kicked out if the information got out. The night that I died, however, I felt that she might've had an inkling about how well I truly knew him. And if she liked him... then...

They sat down on a bench in the courtyard. It was pretty secluded and I could see Jayden breathe out a slight sigh of relief. He didn't handle fame like I thought he would. All throughout middle and high school, Jayden was the cockiest, most arrogant boy I had ever come across. I had thought once he was a famous basketball player, like he had always wanted, that he would eat it up. Get with any girl at any time—which, honestly, he kind of always did anyways—and be at the clubs twenty-four seven. He wasn't ever at the clubs, at least for as long as I've been tethered to him, and he seemed to hate the attention that he would get on the streets or in public.

"So, are you here to talk about Grace?" Valentina asked. "I saw you... at the funeral."

"Yeah, he's here to talk about me," I muttered without thinking. He glanced up at me as if to ask me: *What's your problem?* I shrugged in response and then crossed my arms, a flood of emotions that I couldn't name beating on my chest.

"Yeah-h-h," he said, dragging out the word as his eyes focused back on Valentina. "Did you know she was killed?" Valentina's hazel eyes widened.

"No, no one told me that," she said. She looked genuinely shocked.

"Yeah, the police haven't made that public knowledge, yet... and the autopsy hasn't been finalized either..." Jayden muttered. "But, I'm pretty sure she was poisoned."

"I feel like if you were trying to figure out if she killed me or not, this wouldn't be the way to go about it," I pointed out.

"Whatever," Jayden said.

"Sorry?" Valentina asked. Jayden shook his head as he realized that he just talked aloud to me.

"Uh, nothing," he said, quickly. "Anyways, she obviously drank some wine from a basket of cookies that was delivered to her. And I just have this feeling that she was poisoned. She wouldn't have... killed herself like that." Valentina nodded slowly, obviously taken aback by the conversation.

"No, she wasn't the type to kill herself. And, she didn't have any health problems, from what I know," Valentina said, slowly. She stared at Jayden, as if she were studying him. Jayden shifted uncomfortably in her gaze.

"I didn't know you all were that close," she said. "Honestly, I didn't know you two really knew each other at all. Yet, here you are." Jayden laughed, slightly.

"No, we weren't close. I've just known her for a long time and... I..." he stared up at me as if to ask me for help.

"What? What do you want?" I asked. His large eyes grew bigger as he tried to communicate his thoughts that I could not hear.

"I don't have telepathy powers," I said.

"*You're a ghost,*" he hissed through his teeth. I heard his unvoiced thoughts: *How do you* not *have powers?* Valentina's eyebrows scrunched together.

"That doesn't mean I have powers! Just talk! Pretend I'm not here!" I said, ducking behind Valentina. Jayden blinked slowly as he stared into Valentina's face.

"Is everything okay?" she asked. He tried to laugh off what just happened.

"Yeah, no, everything's good. I'm good," he said. "I just... her *death*, you know... it's been really hard on me." I gave Jayden a thumbs up. He glared at me quickly before looking back at Valentina. Her eyes followed Jayden's gaze, but I could tell she saw straight through me.

"Oh, I thought I saw a spider," Jayden said, saving face.

"A spider?" Valentina shrilled. I laughed as I remembered that she was deathly afraid of spiders. Jayden waved his hands quickly.

"I was mistaken though. It wasn't a spider. I just have really, *really* bad eyesight. I think everything looks like spiders... from a distance," Jayden quickly said. She just blinked at him. He wiped his hands on his sweatpants as he looked around the courtyard.

"Anyways," he said, "It's just been really hard losing Grace. I have a lot of... regrets." It sounded like it took every bit of him to be able to say that lie. I laughed silently from behind Valentina.

"I'm just trying to figure out who would want to kill her," he finished, quickly.

"To be honest," Valentina said, running a hand through her hair, "I didn't know Grace all that well. The only people that I would hear her talk about was someone named Will?" Jayden nodded.

"Yeah, Will and I are best friends," he said. Will and *him* were best friends? He was delusional.

"And her therapist," she finished. Jayden's thick eyebrow raised.

"Therapist?" he said.

"You didn't know she talked to one? It was weird. I've had a therapist before but... they didn't call me on the phone like hers does," she said. Then, she shrugged. "But, she said since they can't see each other in person, she has a lot of video sessions or quick phone calls."

"A therapist, huh?" Jayden said, more to himself.

"Everyone sees a therapist these days. It's not that weird," I pointed out.

"No, but when did she start seeing this therapist?" he asked. Valentina shrugged.

"I don't know. She never told me," she responded. But I knew this was Jayden's way of indirectly asking me.

"I started seeing him before my mom died. When I was around sixteen," I answered, quickly. Jayden nodded, as if he were nodding to Valentina's response.

"There's no one that you know that would want to hurt Grace," Jayden affirmed. Valentina thought for a moment and then she snapped her fingers.

"Actually," she said, "Greg asked her out that night. I'm sure of it."

"Who's Greg?" Jayden asked. Valentina stared at him for a moment.

"He works at the stadium," she said. Jayden's face remained blank. "He's one of the guys who wipes down the court."

"Oh-h-h," Jayden said, sounding out the syllable. But I could tell from his eyes that he still didn't know who she was talking about. Valentina waved his words away.

"Anyways," she continued, "He remembered her birthday, gave her a card, and after the game, I saw him talking to her. It looked like he was asking her out, but she was fixated on you. You gave her a *lot* of anxiety that night." Jayden squinted his eyes as he thought for a moment.

"It's the guy that I was talking to when you came out of the locker room to glare at me and then walked away," I clarified.

"Oh-h-h!" Jayden exclaimed, finally remembering Greg, though I felt like he was remembering the wrong person. "Oh, man, I know that dude. He was asking Grace out? Of all people? He knows there's dancers that would go out with him, right?" I rolled my eyes.

"He definitely was asking her out and it looked like she rejected him. He also gave me some weird vibes," Valentina said.

"That's a motive," Jayden pointed out.

"If he was crazy enough to, yeah," she said. Jayden nodded as he made eye contact with me.

* * *

"It's not Greg," I said as Jayden slathered lotion onto his face. He rubbed it into his cheeks as he stared knowingly at me. I rolled my eyes as I turned away from his gaze. I had been watching him rub lotion into his face, just lotion, every night for the past week and it was incredibly frustrating. Why didn't he have a better skincare routine?

"You should put more than just lotion on," I said. It had to be the thousandth time I've told him this.

"Lotion is all I need," he, once again, responded. I tried to leave his presence, but I just teleported back in front of him. This had to be hell. It really did. Jayden didn't react to my reappearing as he stared at me through the mirror.

"How do you know it wasn't Greg? Don't girls talk all the time about how they're afraid to reject a guy or something because of murder or other stuff?" Jayden said vaguely, continuing to rub the lotion in.

"He's a nice guy and he wasn't really trying to ask me out, I don't think," I said the last part quietly. I tried to remember what he was saying at that moment.

"Yeah, internalized misogyny *is* your problem," Jayden said as he turned away.

"What do you mean?" I asked. He raised an eyebrow.

"You thought that Valentina killed you, your only friend that's a girl, and you don't think this random dude murdered you?"

"I told you that I didn't think she killed me," I muttered. The other eyebrow raised.

"You for sure wondered if she murdered you," he said. It bothered me that he was saying that I had internalized misogyny. Maybe I did, but I didn't want Jayden to be throwing that back at my face.

"I already said it might've been internalized misogyny," I mumbled. Jayden turned back around to face me.

"What did he say to you?" Jayden asked.

"Who? Greg? He said 'I was wondering if you wanted to...'" I repeated the words that he said and then quickly continued, "But, that didn't necessarily mean he wanted to go on a date with me. It could've been a 'I was wondering if you wanted to sweep the floor right now because I'm busy and I have a really eventful night with some of the dancers on the dance team and I just don't have time' kind of thing." Jayden looked at me like I was a lunatic.

"What?" I asked.

"That definitely was *not* what he was asking. Have you never talked to a man before in your life?" Jayden asked as he started to get into bed. It was starting to get normal to see him sleep, even though I would turn around for the whole night. Luckily, he was still wearing pajamas to bed, due to me not being able to leave and everything.

"I've talked to you and Will," I pointed out.

"No, I mean, like, as a man," he said, shaking his head.

"No," I said quietly, surprised that I was admitting this to him. His eyebrows raised as he looked over at me. He looked surprised. Why did *he* look surprised?

"Anyways," I said, changing the subject, "It can't be Greg." Jayden stared at me for a moment. It felt like his eyes were piercing through me, and I knew if I had blood rushing through my body, I would be blushing. Or was I already, anyways? Blushing because of how uncomfortable it made me. *Of course.*

"Why are you so sure it isn't Greg? If he asked you

out, and you rejected him, and he's *tripping*, he might try and kill you," Jayden pointed out.

"Yeah, but by sending a nice basket of treats? I just feel like if a guy is that upset, wouldn't he just stab me?" I said. I had watched a lot of crime documentaries and a cookie basket wasn't one that men seemed to use all that often.

"That's why you thought it was Valentina," Jayden said, nodding his head. "Because you think a girl would send an edible arrangement, not a dude, even though she doesn't really have a motive." *Yeah, Jayden,* I couldn't help but think to myself, *maybe it* wasn't *internalized misogyny.*

"Well, I did think it was you at first," I pointed out.

"But not anymore," he said, but with a slight lilt in his voice that made it seem like he was asking.

"The jury is still out on that one," I retorted, but I felt myself smile a little.

ten

I LAID down next to Jayden on the bed, who was sprawled out on his back. His limbs were incredibly long and I wondered how he even fit on his bed. I picked up one of his arms, surprised that I could hold it, and then threw it onto his stomach. He groaned and rolled over to his side, facing me.

I couldn't sleep anymore. Death was just a waking nightmare. Time was just ticking away slower than a sloth climbing up to the top of a tree. Even though sleep wasn't going to come for me, I would still lay next to Jayden. Sometimes I would stand over him, in hopes that he would wake up and scream. Tonight, though, I was exhausted. I didn't really feel like haunting him. Was it really possible that Greg, the seemingly sweet guy who worked at the stadium, poisoned me? I shook my head. A basket of cookies wasn't the normal way to try and murder someone. And a lot of thought ahead of time had to have been put in. A guy who was spurned not even an hour before? I just didn't think it could be him.

I stared at Jayden's face as I thought. His mouth was slightly open. Snores quietly rumbling out through his lips. When he slept, his face looked angry, like he was arguing with someone in his dreams constantly. I turned over onto my back. He was most likely arguing with his dad, or me.

In the quiet of Jayden's bedroom, I thought about the times I've met James King, Jayden's dad. I could count on one hand how many times I had, including the one time I went over to Jayden's house.

Will had the bright idea, senior year of high school, that Jayden, him, and I should form a study group to study for the AP Literature exam. I, personally, was just surprised that Jayden was even in AP Lit in the first place, considering he didn't strike me as the kind of guy who liked to read and analyze those readings. He seemed like one of those people who would tweet out that English teachers read too much into books. For example, an English teacher might think that the eyes in *The Great Gatsby* represent the eyes of God, but perhaps the author just put in that detail just for detail sake. I didn't particularly care either way. Maybe the author intended for it to have a greater meaning, maybe they didn't. The crazier the interpretation that I could think of, as well as prove, the higher my grade was. So I liked to read into stories.

Anyways, Jayden just didn't seem like the kind of

person who would be into literature, so, at the time, I jumped at the opportunity to see him in this light.

His house was in a gated neighborhood. It had a fancy Italian name that I couldn't possibly name now, but if you wanted to go into the neighborhood, you had to press a button at the gate and give the name of the person you were seeing. The voice in the black box had a list of names that were allowed to visit, and if your name wasn't on the list, you weren't coming in. Luckily, Jayden didn't abandon me and had put me on the list that day. And the gates flew wide open.

The houses in this neighborhood were massive. They almost looked like castles and they were spread fairly far apart from one another. I caught glimpses of beautiful backyards with huge, expensive patios and glistening, crystal blue pools. I wasn't surprised that Jayden was rich. He wore sneakers that were more expensive than my parents' mortgage. But, it was unreal seeing these houses.

I drove down the winding road and eventually my GPS told me that I had arrived at his house. I parked my car on his stone driveway and just looked up at it, awed. It really looked like a castle, almost Victorian. I felt my jaw just drop. But, I quickly picked it back up as the double doors opened.

I had never seen James King in person before. He was darker than Jayden and maybe a bit taller, but it was hard to gauge considering I was the size of one of his legs. He looked upset as he turned around, with Jayden ducking through the doors.

"Will you explain to me what your coach said?" Mr. King asked. Jayden's head was down. I had never seen him look so... solemn before.

"There's no explanation," Jayden had muttered.

"So you walked off the court for no reason?" Mr. King asked. His voice was calm, but it felt menacing. Jayden had stayed quiet. I had heard that during practice the other day, Jayden walked off the court because the coach told him to stop hogging the ball, or something to that effect. He had cussed out his coach, cussed out his teammates, basically said he was better than all of them, and then walked off. He didn't return to practice.

"You beat up your teammates last year, and now this year you won't play with them? Talent means nothing if you can't handle yourself," Jayden's father said after a long moment of silence. My eyebrows raised at Mr. King's words. I never heard of him beating up his teammates. Mr. King started to walk back into the house, but then he took his large hand and hit Jayden over the side of his head. I jumped at the noise.

"I better not hear something like this again," he ordered. He turned around and paused, "You don't even have enough talent to be acting like this." Then, he walked back into the house and Jayden just stood there, for a moment. He just stared at the stone driveway for what felt like forever. I didn't move an inch, didn't breathe, hoping that he wouldn't notice I was there. Then, his head turned slightly to the side, and he looked at me. We stared at each other for a long while. I didn't know what to say or do.

Jayden didn't even look surprised that I was there. His eyes held me in that spot, frozen, as I waited for him to say something, anything. But, he just stared. Eventually, he turned around and walked back into his house, closing the double doors behind him.

I waited there, on his driveway, until Will came. We never talked about what happened between him and his dad. It was the only time I think I ever saw them talk to one another. After that occurrence, I would always look to see if his dad was at Jayden's games. But, he never was.

Looking at Jayden's sleeping face, I wondered if they talked at all after that last game, where he got kicked out. Where *I* kicked him out. I sighed quietly to myself.

"I'm sorry," I whispered towards Jayden's face, only able to apologize to him due to him being uncon-scious. His eyebrows were still scrunched up as he slept, arguing with whoever he was arguing with.

"I'm sorry," I repeated as I pressed a finger to the point where his eyebrows almost met. At my touch, they relaxed slightly.

eleven

JAYDEN WOKE UP, flailing, which promptly scared me out of my daydream.

"What? What is it?" I asked as he rolled over and grabbed something from his pillow. His phone was vibrating and on the screen read "Mia." *Oh shit.*

"Hello?" he said, groggily. All I heard on the other side was screaming. Mia was Jayden's ex-girlfriend. I had only heard of her from Will, but she had a lot of insecurities while dating Jayden. Understandably so. Her boyfriend was a professional basketball player and there were girls that threw themselves at basketball players, taken or not. But, from what I understood of their breakup, Jayden was still in love with her. However, all Will told me at the time was that Mia couldn't handle Jayden's friendships, in love or not.

"Mia? Mia? I'm gonna hang up," Jayden said over her yelling. "You're tripping right now. Tripping." He promptly hung up the phone and rubbed his forehead, before placing his brown eyes on my face.

"It's Mia," he said, lying back down on his bed. Then, he made a face as he looked me up and down, like he smelled something bad.

"What are you doing on my bed?" he asked. I stared at him as I tried to think of some kind of excuse.

"Uh," I said, as I looked up to the ceiling. I tried to think of anything to say, but my mind went blank.

"Do ghosts sleep or something?" he asked. I nodded my head, thankful for the reason.

"Yeah, and I just didn't want to sleep on the floor again. It isn't comfortable," I partially lied. Jayden nodded slowly, as he thought to himself. He laid back into his giant black pillow.

"So, Mia," I said slowly. Jayden's eyes widened.

"Oh yeah," he said, taking out his phone once again. He started tapping on the screen, rapidly, writing something into the search bar.

"She said something about an article..." his voice drifted off as his eyes focused onto the screen. His eyes moved back and forth as he read.

"What article? What is she talking about?" I asked. He laid his head back onto his pillow as he put a hand over his eyes.

"They think we might've been dating," he muttered. "Like, we were seeing each other on and off."

"US?" I asked, flabbergasted. He just nodded, his

hand still over his eyes, but the tips of his ears reddened.

"Why would they think that *we* were dating?" I asked. But also, why would Mia care if we were?

"Secretly dating," he added.

"Secretly? On and off?" I asked. I couldn't wrap my head around what he was talking about. Motioning towards his phone, I leaned in.

"Show me the article," I quickly demanded. I couldn't hold his phone in my own hands, since I was dead. So, Jayden turned his phone towards me as I took his wrist to pull it closer, in order to see it better. I was surprised that a jolt ran up my arms and down my spine, but I tried to ignore it. I didn't have *feelings* for Jayden—it was impossible. It was just being stuck with him, that was all. *Stockholm syndrome*, I thought to myself.

The headline read: "Basketball Player Jayden King Secretly Dating Deceased Referee?" I scrunched up my face at how they referred to me and then continued to read the rest of the article.

According to a high school friend of theirs, they were always near each other and arguing like a married couple. "It was obvious they were dating, from day one. Everyone thought so," Shyla, King's classmate, told The Foul. "They would have hushed conversations in the hallway all the time. I even have a picture of them holding hands." And there, in the article, was a picture of Jayden's and I's hands held together, but...

"This was *completely* taken out of context!" I

shouted, as I threw his arms towards him. His phone hit his chest.

"Ow," he said.

"We weren't holding hands because we were *dating*. We held hands for, like, a *second* because you grabbed it as I was walking away from you," I continued to yell. Jayden winced as he put a finger to his ear.

"Yo, could you stop yelling please?" he said, closing his eyes. I sat there, on his bed, fuming.

"I can't believe anyone would think that we were dating and... Shyla??" I said, gesturing towards his phone. "She barely knew us. How did she even take a picture of that one miserable millisecond!"

"Okay, we both know that second was the best second of your life," Jayden said, laughing a little. "I mean—" His eyes scanned my face and he promptly shut up.

"I cannot believe my reputation is tainted like this. Forever. After my death," I whispered to myself.

"*Your* reputation? People think I dated a... grungy... What *was* the look you were going for all the time?" he asked. I just stared at him. He cleared his throat quickly.

"Anyways, people think I dated a referee, which is probably against protocol," his eyes widened as that last part dawned on him. His head turned towards me suddenly. "Do you think I'll get kicked out of the league?" I shook my head as I got off of his bed.

"No," I said, "Because you have Will as a witness

and no one would believe it. The Foul is just a stupid sports tabloid."

"Mia believed it," Jayden said slowly.

"Why *would* Mia believe it?" I asked, curiosity coating my tongue. "We weren't even talking then. Like, at all." I had cut off Jayden periodically in my life and before he had started dating Mia was one of those times. It was actually when he first got drafted into the NBA. I was incredibly upset at the time. I was worried that I wouldn't have the chance to officiate in the league because we knew each other. Or, maybe, I was just jealous. Either way, I was told I should stop talking to him, even on a cordial basis. So, I did.

"How did Mia even know about me?" I asked, looking at him. His face had stiffened and he just looked at his phone, scrolling through Bleacher Report.

"I don't know," he muttered. "Maybe Will." Then, he put down his phone, angrily, as he got up from his bed and walked towards the bathroom. It felt like I was being dragged as my feet slowly followed him for a couple of steps. I could almost feel the string that was attaching us together. My hands reached for it, almost touching the invisible prison. *If only I could cut it.*

Jayden started brushing his teeth vigorously. His eyebrows were low on his face and if looks could kill, I'd be dead twice over by now. What he was upset about, I couldn't guess.

"Is this about Mia?" I pried, even though I probably shouldn't have.

"Is what about Mia?" he asked, his voice deadpan.

"Your mood," I pointed out.

"What mood?"

"Oh my God," I whispered, blowing hair out of my face. My hair was forever down now, and there wasn't any way to put it up in a ponytail anymore. We stared each other down for a moment through the mirror.

"You're *such* a child," I mumbled. He turned around to stare at me, as if I had betrayed him in some way, and I felt my face soften. His jaw tightened as he turned back towards the sink and splashed his face with water. He, then, walked out of the bathroom, his face wet.

"What did I do?" I asked, unable to cope with his anger. It gave me this building anxiety, just being around him when he was like that. I hated feeling like I was walking on eggshells around him, worried about saying the littlest thing. He went from this warm, joking boy—someone who had the sun's adoration on them at all times—to this cold, stone-like person. The statue was who I had come to see most, growing up, while the sun was the person I could only see from afar. And I always wondered why it was me. Why did *I* always somehow turn him into stone?

"You didn't do anything," Jayden sighed, grabbing a protein drink from the refrigerator.

"I did say or do something," I muttered. His eyes

pierced through me as he started to drink. He put the cup down after a while, his gaze almost softening.

"You didn't do anything," he whispered. "It's my fault." Then, he looked away and I could breathe again. Before I could inquire further, a banging came from his front door.

"Jayden Anthony King, I know you're in there," the voice yelled out. Jayden looked like he wanted to hide underneath a table.

"You better not try to hide from me, Jayden, or I swear to God I'll—" she then proceeded to describe how she'd cut him up into tiny pieces and feed him to her dog in surprisingly graphic detail. Jayden stared at me as he slowly walked over to the door.

"Mia stresses me out sometimes, okay? So don't say anything or I might respond to you in front of her and we both don't want that," he whispered.

"Who are you talking to in there?" Mia shouted. His eyes widened as he started to open the door. She put her foot in the gap that he created and pushed her way in.

"Who's in here?" she asked, her hands on her hips. Mia was, in a word, breathtaking. She was slightly darker than Jayden, but unlike Jayden, she was mixed. Half Chinese and half Black, and her features definitely showed that. Her eyes were slightly upturned, though her face shape is what gave her away. It was distinctly southern China. V-shaped jaw, apple cheeks, and a high forehead. Her dark brown, tight curls were pulled away from her face in a high ponytail and when she glared up at Jayden, she still couldn't help but look cute. I envied her. I envied how effortlessly beautiful she was. No wonder why Jayden was still in love with her.

"No one is in here," Jayden said as he followed her around his apartment. She looked all around his large apartment as Jayden continued to repeat that no one was here. She pointed a finger into his face.

"I heard you talking to someone," she said.

"Mia," Jayden sighed, "I was talking to myself, okay? I do that sometimes." Her nose scrunched up, making her look like a chipmunk.

"You do not talk to yourself," she said.

"It's been a long time since we dated. People change," Jayden said, his voice monotone. She stared at him, as if recognizing how long it had been since they had seen each other. The silence was uncomfortable, as they measured each other up. Finally, she adjusted her clothes and walked towards the kitchen. Sitting on a bar stool, she pulled out her phone.

"Explain this article," she said. It was the one that she was yelling about on the phone earlier. Jayden sighed as he leaned down on his counter. The counter was custom made so that it wouldn't be too short for him.

"We weren't dating," Jayden said. "Grace and I have never dated. She has always hated my guts." Then, he paused for a moment, his eyes glancing towards me. "Had." He looked down. Mia stared at him for a moment.

"Then why would a classmate say—"

"Shyla has always been really bad with gossip and while she was dating my friend Will, she tried to kiss me at a party one time. I rejected her, so she's always had some vendetta against me," Jayden explained. My eyebrows raised to my hairline.

"Shyla tried to *kiss* you? In high school?" I asked. Jayden tried his hardest not to glare at me to stop talking.

"I think she made up that whole thing with Grace because it was the only explanation that she could wrap her puny head around as to why I didn't want to be with her," Jayden muttered. I knew that the explanation was for me, but he did a good job in making it seem like it was just more explanation for Mia.

"Then what about—"

"The picture?" Jayden guessed. He sighed again as he shifted uncomfortably. He looked like he wanted to die having this conversation. *I* wanted to die listening to this conversation. It was embarrassing that people actually believed that we were dating. Jayden and *I?* I would have to be dead before anything would happen between us. Well, dead again. I would have to die like a thousand times before I would have feelings for Jayden King.

"I held her hand, I think, one time in all the years that I've known her. She's always had a thing about being touched. Anyway, we had this really big argument. It was stupid. And Grace wasn't letting me explain, so I grabbed her hand before she could walk away. It was for a second and I seriously don't know how Shyla took a picture of that, honest," Jayden said. His hand moved closer to Mia's, as if he wanted to grab hers, but he closed it into a fist and pulled it away. I noticed that her eyes glanced down at the motion, but neither of them mentioned it.

"What was the argument about?" Mia asked, after a while, one eyebrow raised.

"Honestly?" Jayden said, "I don't want to talk about it." Mia's lips tightened as she grabbed her purse, pointing another finger into Jayden's face. She walked up closer to him.

"You were always so tight-lipped about that Grace. Our *whole* relationship," she hissed.

"I was not—" She shook her head.

"You were. You were always mentioning her. Upset about her. But, you would never talk in depth about her. Like she was some kind of secret that you were keeping close to your heart," she accused. I felt my own heart stop. *What did she mean?* My eyes glanced over at Jayden's face, which had stiffened. He had shut down. A statue, once again. Because of me.

"She's dead, Mia," Jayden said. "I'm not going to talk about her. Not now." Mia glared up at him for a moment longer and then shook her head.

"I could never compete with her," she whispered, more to herself than anything. "She always brought out all of your emotions, and all you ever were was polite to me."

"I loved you, Mia," Jayden hissed. "And all you

cared about was someone that you never met and someone that I wasn't even talking to at the time."

"I *know* you weren't talking to her, Jayden!" she yelled out. "The fact that she cut you off was all that you *could* talk about. Our whole relationship revolved around her. You *loved* me?" She shook her head as she backed away, her eyes starting to well up with tears. Swallowing them down, she looked away.

"When are you ever going to admit it to yourself?" she whispered, not daring to look at Jayden. Jayden just stared at her, and I had never seen him look so helpless.

"She's dead, and you still can't admit it," she muttered, before grabbing the doorknob. She waited a moment, her back turned towards Jayden, waiting for him to say something, anything. But he just stared at her. What he was thinking, I couldn't tell. In silence, she walked out of the door. And I was left with a whirlwind of emotions swirling around in my head.

twelve

WE DIDN'T SPEAK about what Mia said after she left. A part of me wanted to, wanted to know what she was talking about. I wanted to know what she was implying, and if what she was implying matched what I had in my head. But, I wasn't going to say it out loud. I wasn't even going to think it.

After Mia left, Jayden just hung his head in silence. It looked like he was going through his thoughts and I didn't know what to say. He looked... heartbroken. I had heard from Will that he was truly in love with Mia. The first woman that he dated that he ever really had deep feelings for. And standing here, watching his heart break again, I could see that he was genuine in his feelings for her. Something in my chest ached, watching him. It really felt like I was a ghost, for the first time.

I shook my head. This *had* to be Stockholm Syndrome. I was stuck with Jayden, unable to leave his side. So, *of course* I was starting to care for him a little. I nodded my head. *Yeah, that's it.*

"You still remember that fight?" I asked, clearing my throat after a while. Jayden's eyes glanced at me and he laughed a little, coming out of his statue-like state.

"How can I forget it?" he almost whispered. Then, he cleared his throat. "You were so mad at me."

"I was always mad at you," I pointed out. He nodded as his eyes glazed over from the memory. Honestly, I was surprised he even remembered that fight. It didn't seem that big of a deal to him at the time. Just another joke or just another fight with me. He didn't seem to care.

"Yeah, but this was different," he said, slowly. He was right. That fight was different for me. It was also the first time I cut Jayden out of my life.

We were juniors in high school at the time, and my mom had just passed away a month ago. It was close to the end of the year and I was walking down the hall towards my locker. That's when I heard it. The rumor that Jayden started about me.

"That's her," one of the girls whispered as I walked by. They seemed to giggle to one another as I felt my face burn. Were they talking about me? I continued down towards my locker and waiting there was Will. His face was downcast and I knew that he had bad news to tell me.

"What's up?" I asked, pointedly. He looked at me and shrugged, running a hand through his wavy blonde hair. His gray eyes avoided mine. I stared into the abyss that was the inside of my locker.

"I heard some girls whispering about me. So," I said, turning towards him, "*What* is up?"

"In the locker room the other day," Will started. He stopped talking as some boys walked behind us. I watched his eyes, as he glared.

"Can you stop with the suspense?" I asked, sarcastically. "It's killing me."

"Jayden said some stuff in the locker room yesterday at practice," Will said slowly. I narrowed my eyes.

"I'm guessing it was about me," I muttered. Will nodded. I took a deep breath as I prepared for the nonsense that Jayden said about me. It couldn't possibly be worse than the time where he said that he thought I looked like an elf mixed with an ogre. Everyone called me "Elgre" for all of freshman year.

"What did he say?" I asked, as it was obvious that Will wasn't going to delve into it further.

"He said something about how you're obsessed with him," Will whispered. I frowned. That wasn't enough to warrant the school spreading rumors about me.

"What else was said?" I asked. I thought to myself for a moment.

"Were you there? When whatever was said happened?" I asked, pointedly. Will shook his head.

"I couldn't go to practice yesterday. I had a doctor's appointment. So, what I'm about to tell you is just coming from what I've heard. I don't know if it's entirely true or not," Will explained. I motioned towards him to get a move on.

"Just tell me, Will," I said. He took a deep breath.

"Jayden said something about how you were so obsessed with him. One of the other guys then started talking about... Asian... uh..." Will paused. I felt my face start to burn. Any time a guy starts talking specifically about Asians, it wasn't necessarily a good conversation.

"What did he talk about?" I asked, almost robotically.

"He said Asian girls... their... it's slanted," Will stammered. He was obviously uncomfortable about the conversation and I felt the embarrassment bubble up in my chest. Will continued on, quickly.

"The guys started talking about how it would... feel and stuff like that. They told Jayden that he should try you out sometime. He apparently laughed, but I don't think he said anything more. The guys then continued to talk about some... disturbing stuff. Really disturbing stuff," Will said.

"What did they say?" I asked, through gritted teeth. One hand was on the door to my locker, my knuckles white. Will swallowed.

"They said something about how naive you were, how you would willingly follow them somewhere and they could... take advantage... of the situation," Will said, quietly. "They said they want to try out an Asian's... yeah." While Will was doing his best to censor the situation, I got the gist of it. I gripped the locker door, hard, as I stared into it. My eyes were burning and I was trying hard to slow the racing of my heart. I felt... scared and *violated*. I had heard that stereotype before. But that's what it was, a stereotype. It was frustrating that people believed it... to a violent degree.

"Where's Jayden?" I asked, my jaw clenched.

"Grace, he didn't say—"

"Where. Is. Jayden?" I seethed. Will hung his head.

"He's getting ready for practice. But, after those guys said that, he—" he started, but I tuned him out. The thought of talking to Jayden, in front of all those guys, made me feel like throwing up. I hated them. I hated *all* of them.

I turned on my heel, slamming my locker door shut, as I walked down the hallway. Even though my heart was pounding, I wasn't going to let them scare me into not saying anything. I opened the locker room door to the protests of the boys inside. Scanning the room for Jayden, I made eye contact with him and then beckoned him over. His comically large eyes looked confused at my expression. Jayden quietly followed me out of the locker room and once we were outside, I was so angry; I couldn't even look at him.

"Grace, if this is about—"

"It is," I said, flatly. Jayden stared at me for a moment.

"Listen, I just—"

"You just *listened*," I finished for him, my eyes

flashing at him. He took a step back at my expression. The confusion written all over his face made me want to scream.

"You just *stood there* and listened," I said. "Not only that, you *laughed*." He scrunched his face up at that.

"Listen, I don't know who told you—"

"No," I fumed, glaring at him, "*You* listen. You're the most *despicable*, worthless, piece of shit that I've *ever* met. You will amount to *nothing,* you stupid, lowlife douchebag." His face fell at my words as I turned around, swiftly. I could feel my body start to shake and I just wanted to leave his presence as soon as possible. But, before I could get far enough, Jayden grabbed my hand. I turned my head to look at it, every part of my body felt like bugs were crawling all over it at his touch.

"Grace, I'm sorry. I was just saying that you were obsessed with me and it went too far. I'm sorry and I made sure that it'll never—"

"You'll never let it happen again?" I felt my anger bubble over as I ripped my hand out from his grip. "*You're* the one who cultivated this conversation. You always talk shit about me to them. And they got so... comfortable that it turned into this violent, disgusting conversation." My whole body was visibly shaking now and I could tell that Jayden noticed. It was obvious that he didn't know what to do.

"Grace—" He looked confused and... frustrated.

"Fuck you, Jayden. *Never* speak to me again," I

hissed, before turning away. He didn't try to stop me that time.

Remembering that fight made my chest hurt. That was one of the most miserable times of my life. And it must've been obvious that I was remembering it as Jayden hovered a hand over my shoulder, as if he were debating whether he should place it there or not. He eventually did and it took everything in me not to shrug it off.

"I *am* really sorry about that time, Grace," Jayden whispered.

"It was a long time ago," I mumbled. "It's fine."

"No, it's not. I shouldn't have even started talking about you in the first place," Jayden said. I stared at him and remembered what Will had told me multiple times afterwards.

"You know," I said, "Will kept trying to convince me that wasn't why people were talking about me. It was because you told them off and hit the guy who said that about me." I laughed slightly at the thought of Jayden defending my honor. But, the sound was bitter. Jayden would never do anything like that. As I laughed, though, I saw his face turn slightly red. My laughter faded as I stared at him.

"Wait, did you actually...?" Jayden cleared his throat.

"You never let me explain. You just assumed that I went along with the conversation and then never spoke to me again. Any time I tried to explain after that, you would just tell me off or walk away," Jayden muttered. I stared at him, in shock.

"This whole time I thought..." I said slowly. His gaze looked fiery as he remembered the conversation.

"I punched Allen in the mouth for saying what he did," Jayden said. "Luckily, I didn't get suspended for it since he lied about how he got that black eye." I remembered seeing Allen walking around with his eye almost swollen shut and a bruise on his cheek. He also never spoke to me again after that, when usually he would make a few snide remarks here or there. My eyes met Jayden's. He... protected me? *Jayden* did? All these years I thought that he laughed at the conversation, at my pain, but instead he stopped it from continuing. Was everything I knew about him a lie?

"Why didn't anyone tell me?" I asked, softly. He stared at me as if I should've already known the answer.

"You stopped talking to everyone after your mom died. And since you weren't speaking to me, you weren't speaking to Will either. No one could've told you because you wouldn't let anyone close enough to you," he muttered. "Plus, I didn't really want you to know." Jayden was right. My only friend was Will, and I stopped hanging out with him after this incident with Jayden. No matter how many times he tried to talk to me about it, I would ignore him.

"Is that why you didn't tell Mia about our fight? Because I was right here, listening, and you didn't want me to know?" Jayden shrugged.

"That's so childish," I pointed out. He shrugged again and then leaned against the counter. He looked at me, as if he were searching for something in my expression.

"What?" I asked. He shook his head.

"I just... You never talked about it with me. Not even after we started talking again," he said. "Didn't you want to hear my side?" I shrugged.

"What was the point? You weren't my friend," I said. "I hated you and you letting people talk about me like that just seemed normal. Like, you *would* let a conversation like that happen."

"Ouch," he said, holding a hand over his heart, "That hurts."

"It's just how you were to me," I pointed out. "So, why would I talk to you about it? I wasn't trying to fix anything." Jayden stared at me for a moment. Then, he nodded.

"Right, we weren't friends," he said, mostly to himself. He, then, smiled up at me, but his smile didn't quite reach his eyes. "You hated me."

"You hated me, too," I pointed out. Although a small part of me, a hopeful part of me, thought maybe he didn't hate me as much as I thought he did. But, he nodded, as he started walking back into his bedroom.

"I did," he said, shattering that hope. "I definitely did."

thirteen

I WATCHED as Jayden tightened his shoes. He was getting ready for practice, and I just had to be dragged up and down the court due to this ghostly string that held us together. I was starting to be able to see it, but no matter how many times I tried to break it, it wasn't budging. I stared at the length of the court. *This was going to be fun*, I thought sarcastically to myself.

"Shyla tried to kiss you?" I asked. "While she was dating Will?"

"I don't really want to talk about this," Jayden muttered under his breath, looking around to see if anyone was near him. His lips barely moved as he talked.

"I just can't believe that happened. Did you ever tell Will?" I asked, as he tightened his other shoe. He quickly shook his head.

"No?" I asked.

"No," he said, his jaw clenched.

"Why wouldn't you tell Will? I thought he was your best friend. You let Will date a girl that was into you the whole time? That isn't fair to—"

"I *got* it, G," Jayden whispered. Putting my hands on my hips, I stared down at him as he stared up at me.

"You need to tell him," I said, "Or at some point, I will put myself into his dreams and tell him myself."

"Can you do that?" he asked. I shrugged.

"I might be able to. You never know," I warned. Jayden narrowed his eyes at me as he measured up what I was saying. I stared back at him.

"What are you looking at, bro?" asked Jayden's teammate Tre as he stared at me, and then continued to look up towards the ceiling. "Is there something up there?" Jayden's face had a slight red tinge to it as he looked back down at his shoes.

"Nah, man, I was just praying," Jayden murmured. Tre's eyes widened.

"Praying? I didn't know you was a Godly man," Tre said, surprised. Jayden shrugged.

"My friend just died," was Jayden's excuse for everything lately. Tre nodded, his facial expression quickly morphing into pity. Trevonne Smith was one of the guards on the Washington Wolves. He wasn't a great player, but he wasn't that bad either. Every inter-action I ever had with Tre, while living, was a pleasant one. He was one of the nicest guys on the team.

"How are you doing with that? I saw that article this morning about how you and the ref were—"

"We *weren't* dating," Jayden interrupted. "We were just friends. Barely friends. We were like siblings."

"Nice save," I muttered. A part of me felt bothered, like there was a pain in my neck from his explanation. I shook the feeling off. Tre's eyebrows were raised at Jayden's quick explanation.

"Seem a *bit* defensive," he said, pinching his fingers together. Jayden pushed himself off of the bench as he went to go warm up.

"Not defensive," he said, "Just annoyed at the assumptions." Tre passed Jayden the ball as Jayden started practicing some free throws.

"Did you know her for a long time?" Tre asked. Jayden glanced over at me and laughed a little to himself.

"What?" I asked. He just continued to laugh as Tre looked at him like he had lost it.

"I've known her since the sixth grade," Jayden said. "I remember seeing her for the first time, too." I stared at him, for a moment. He remembered the first time he met me? I didn't even really remember the very first time I met him. I knew it had to have been the first day of school, but the only time I remember meeting him, really, was at Will's house later in the year.

"That's a long time," Tre said, throwing another ball in Jayden's direction. Jayden laughed as he tried to shoot the ball. It missed, but Jayden didn't seem to care.

"Yeah, she walked in wearing this over-sized zip-up sweatshirt. It was bright red and she was wearing gray sweatpants. She looked like she was about to go on a run. I remember thinking to myself, like, what was wrong with this girl?" Jayden avoided my gaze as he laughed some more to himself.

"You know," he pointed at Tre as he passed the ball to him, "Girls usually dress up on the first day of school. Grace just looked like she rolled out of bed. It was like she was purposefully trying to look as ugly as she could, to keep everyone away from her. Prickly from the very first day. Should've dressed like a cactus, honestly." I made a face at him as I tried to distance myself. I didn't think I should be hearing this conversation. His words felt offensive, but his tone seemed warm. It confused me on how I was supposed to feel in this moment, that's for sure.

"We met in Mrs. Viper's class. It was English or Language Arts. Whatever they called it back then," his eyes were glazed over as he remembered. "Mrs. Viper asked if anyone read the books on the summer reading list. Everyone knew you didn't have to read that shit. That was just volunteer work, you know? But, Grace was the only person to raise her hand and say that she did. I remember rolling my eyes and thinking that she was going to be hella annoying in this class, bro. And she *was*." Jayden laughed.

"I'm literally standing right here," I finally said, putting my hands on my hips. Jayden glanced over at me, and his face looked... sad for a split second.

"Yeah, she was the bane of my existence for a

while," Jayden muttered. He grabbed the basketball from Tre and continued to practice his free throws.

"Sounds like she made things interesting for you," Tre pointed out. Jayden shrugged.

"She ended up being my best friend's childhood friend, so we had to see each other a lot throughout the years. Will always wanted us to be friends," he muttered.

"You guys never did?" Tre asked. Jayden shrugged one shoulder as he glanced over at me.

"Nah," Jayden said, laughing almost bitterly. He threw the ball, and it went straight into the net. "She hated my guts 'til the bitter end."

* * *

"I didn't hate you until my death," I said, after he finished his practice. He raised his eyebrows at me as he guzzled down a bottle of water. Someone handed him another bottle of water, which he downed as well.

"I didn't!" I insisted. When the person left to give other players water, he turned towards me.

"You thought I murdered you, Grace," he pointed out.

"That doesn't mean I hated you," I muttered.

"I think it kind of implies it. Plus, you pretty much tell me all the time that you hate me and that being with me after death has felt like hell to you," he whispered. I looked up at the ceiling as I thought. Did I say those things out loud?

"It doesn't matter to me, if you hated me or not," Jayden said, barely above a whisper. He wiped his sweat off with a towel, and then stared at it intensely.

"I mean, it *seemed* like it bothered you earlier when you were talking to—"

"Do you think Greg's here?" Jayden asked, interrupting me. *Tre*, I finished in my head. I guess I misread. He was *obviously* not that cut up about it.

"I don't know. He works here at the stadium," I mumbled. I didn't want him to talk to Greg. I seriously didn't think that Greg was the one who poisoned me. It just didn't seem logical.

"We should talk to him," Jayden said, looking around for him. I watched him look around the stadium, my arms crossed.

"You don't know what he looks like, do you?" I asked, an eyebrow raised. He scoffed and rubbed the back of his head.

"I-I know what he looks like. White guy, right?" Jayden said, somewhat confidently.

"He *is* white, yes," I said.

"Right," Jayden said, smiling at me. "So, just gotta look for a white guy."

"He has brown hair, if that helps," I muttered. He looked at me incredulously.

"Nearly every white guy has brown hair," he said. "That description doesn't really help at all." I rolled my eyes. Eventually, as I looked around the stadium, I spotted Greg. He was grabbing the towels that the players had used in order to put them away. I glanced over at Jayden, wondering if he noticed Greg or not. Jayden's eyes roved right past him. Looking at Greg as he put the towels into a bag, I couldn't help but wonder whether he really was asking me out or not. And if he was, would he really have killed me? All I knew at that moment was that I didn't want Jayden to talk to Greg about it. It would be embarrassing enough to listen to Jayden ask him if he had feelings for me. It would be even more humiliating to hear him accuse Greg of murder, senselessly.

Suddenly, Jayden started to walk forward, a knowing smile on his face. I stared at him in shock as I felt myself getting dragged along with him.

"What are you doing?" I asked.

"You were staring at that guy, wistfully," Jayden whispered, "So he must be Greg."

"Wistfully? I do *not* stare wistfully," I said, indignantly. Jayden's eyebrows raised, but he didn't respond to my denial.

"Greg! Hey! Yo, Greg!" Jayden said, bounding towards this lanky, brunette. He waved his arms to get Greg's attention. He looked shocked that Jayden was even trying to talk to him.

"Jayden?" he asked, staring up at him once Jayden got close.

"You're Greg, right?" he asked. Greg nodded his head, shell-shocked.

"Y-yeah," Greg stammered. He shook his head. "Sorry, I didn't know you knew my name."

"You knew Grace, right?" Jayden got right to the

point. It looked like Greg was getting whiplash from this conversation. He nodded.

"Yeah, I knew her a bit," Greg said.

"She died," Jayden pointed out, staring at him expectantly.

"Are you kidding me? *This* is your strategy?" I said, appalled. Jayden ignored me, still staring down at Greg. Greg was silent for a moment, probably in shock.

"Yeah, I heard she... uh, passed away," Greg said, shifting uncomfortably. Jayden leaned back, slightly, crossing his arms as he looked down at Greg.

"So," Jayden said, obviously unsure of where to go from here. "I think she was murdered."

"Why would you *say* that?" I muttered as I slapped my hand to my face. What in the world is he thinking?

"Murdered?" Greg's thin eyebrows raised slightly, but he didn't look all that surprised.

"You were talking to her, before she died," Jayden accused. Greg's mouth twisted and he looked incredibly uncomfortable.

"What is this? An interrogation?" he somewhat joked. Jayden stared at him seriously. Greg measured up Jayden's expression and then cleared his throat.

"Yeah, I talked to her before and after the game. It was her birthday," Greg said.

"A witness is under the impression that you were feeling Grace," Jayden said, his gaze like steel. I felt anxiety build up in my chest. The air between them was tense, but for a reason that I couldn't pick up on, and it made me want to run far away in the opposite direction.

"Were you guys actually dating or something?" Greg said. His face almost looked disgusted. Jayden scoffed.

"No, we weren't dating. I just have known her for a long time. But, it sounds like *you* wanted to date her, yeah? Did you ask her out and then she reject you or something?" Jayden asked, almost aggressively. Greg frowned at Jayden's words.

"You think I killed her?"

"Wouldn't be the first time a guy murders a girl who said no," Jayden pointed out. Greg stared at Jayden, astounded, and laughed a bit.

"No, I didn't kill Grace, if that's what you're asking," Greg said, going back to putting towels into his bag. He laughed again, his tone false somewhat. Bitter.

"You know, if anyone killed Grace, wouldn't it be you? You're the one who was always yelling at her and stuff. And that night, she looked terrified of you," Greg said, staring Jayden right in the eyes. Jayden looked somewhat taken aback by that information, and Greg was satisfied at the falter in Jayden's expression.

"Yeah, I didn't kill her, dude," Greg said, backing away from Jayden. "But, if someone did, it probably was someone who treated her like you." Greg turned around and walked away as Jayden's hands balled up into fists. Before he could follow him, I grabbed his arm.

"Stop," I said, "It's not worth it." Jayden just glared at Greg's back as he slowly disappeared.

"You were terrified of me that night," Jayden barely whispered. I stared at him and shrugged.

"You're like six foot ten—"

"I'm six foot eight, actually."

"—and way angrier than usual," I continued.

"If the police hear about something like that, *I'm* the one they're going to arrest. And they're going to try to fit me into that narrative as best as possible," Jayden said, turning around to walk towards the locker room.

"Then I guess you should find the person who murdered me before that," I said. Jayden gave me a once-over and then scoffed.

"Yeah," he said, sarcastically adding, "Easy peasy."

fourteen

"YOU REALLY CAN'T THINK of anyone that might hate you enough to kill you," Jayden said, though it sounded more like a question. He threw his gym bag onto his bed and then flopped onto it. We were back at his apartment and no closer to finding out who had poisoned me that night. I shook my head in response.

"Again, I didn't really talk to anyone except you, Will—"

"Valentina and your therapist," Jayden finished. He put a hand to his chin, taking a page out of Will's book.

"Maybe we should look into those people," Jayden said. I frowned.

"You don't think it's Greg anymore?" I asked. Jayden shrugged as he sat up more in his bed, taking his shoes off. My nose scrunched up in distaste. It was so gross that Jayden wore his shoes around his house, especially in his bed sometimes.

"It could've been him, but he didn't really seem like the type to murder someone," Jayden mused. "Though, he *was* defensive."

"You were accusing him of murder," I pointed out. He nodded.

"True," he said.

"It can't be Will because he and I have known each other for so long. There's no reason why he would want to kill me," I said. Jayden shook his head.

"You can't think like that because we don't know what Will might've been thinking in his head," he said. I frowned.

"You think that Will has the ability to kill me?" I asked. Jayden shrugged one shoulder as he got out of bed and walked towards his living room.

"I don't think he *would*, but he might be hiding something that we both don't know," Jayden said.

"What about Valentina?" I asked, putting my hands on my hips. "She seemed to have a thing for you and if she thought that—" Jayden smiled at my words.

"You really think she was feeling me?" Jayden asked. I rolled my eyes.

"Are you serious?" I asked.

"What?" he said, sitting on the couch. I sat down next to him.

"I'm just saying, if she had a thing for you and she thought that you and I had a thing, maybe she would get rid of the competition, literally," I finished. Jayden stared at the TV as he thought.

"I don't know," Jayden said.

"I don't think she would've killed me. She was my only friend who was a girl. But, she's the only one with a motive besides you," I said, quietly. He silently stared at the TV that was playing a reality show. I was surprised that he enjoyed reality shows so much, but it was something that Jayden seemed to watch on the daily.

"What about your therapist?" Jayden said after a while.

"Dr. Adler?" I asked, surprised.

"Yeah," he said, still looking at the screen. His eyes glanced at me for a moment as I tried to think of what to say, and then they went back to the TV.

"I mean," I stammered, "I don't think he would've killed me. He's my *therapist*."

"He?" Jayden said, slightly to himself.

"Yeah-h-h," I said, dragging the word out. What did my therapist being a guy have to do with anything? Jayden paused for a moment.

"Therapists have mental health issues, too," Jayden finally said. "And therapists could definitely kill someone. How'd you say you met him again?" I sighed.

"I started seeing him when my mom was diagnosed with cancer," I said.

"When you were sixteen," Jayden confirmed. I nodded, surprised he remembered that tidbit of information.

"I have continued to see him since. Good therapists are hard to come by," I pointed out.

"You started acting a bit more... withdrawn when

you were sixteen. I thought it was just because of your mom but…" his voice drifted away as he thought. I didn't like the direction the conversation was going in, and anxiety gripped my heart like a claw.

"How old was he?" he asked, after a while.

"What does that have to do with—"

"Can you just answer the question, Grace?" Jayden asked, his voice slightly stern. I raised my eyebrows at his tone.

"Uh, I don't know. Mid-twenties, I guess. He had just started taking on patients," I muttered. Jayden's whole face seemed to frown at that piece of information.

"What?" I asked, anxiety starting to build in my chest. Just thinking about Dr. Adler was making me nervous.

"Has he ever said weird things to you, Grace?" Jayden asked.

"What do you mean?" I insisted.

"Like, I'm just trying to piece some things together, is all. You were around sixteen when you first started seeing him. You stopped talking to a lot of people during that time—not just me," he added that last part before I could interject, "And you have never gone out with a dude before and you're what twenty-four?" I shrugged.

"I don't know what that has to do with anything," I said, defensively. He finally turned towards me, his eyes holding some kind of anger in them. Who it was for, I wasn't sure, but it was directed towards me.

"Grace, just... humor me," he said, almost sighing with his words, like having this conversation with me was some kind of burden. I crossed my arms over my chest, almost as if I were hugging myself.

"I don't think he says weird things to me," I muttered. Jayden's eyebrows raised, as if he didn't believe me. I hated that look.

"He was my therapist. Just because I met him when I was sixteen and I haven't dated anyone doesn't mean it's my therapist's fault and that he killed me," I insisted. I felt the anger start to build up in my chest, intermingling with my anxiety.

"Dr. Adler is a good guy. He's better than *you*. He's helped me with so much and he's been there for me through everything," I continued. "What do you even know, Jayden?" He put his hands up defensively as he backed away from me, letting the couch swallow him up.

"I wasn't saying anything, but you're getting awfully defensive," Jayden pointed out, a smirk almost playing on his lips. It made me want to punch him in the face.

"I'm not getting—"

"Obviously he must've said something or you wouldn't be freaking out like this," Jayden interrupted.

"Urgh!" I screamed, almost pulling my hair out. "You won't even let me speak for a *second*! You always have to hear yourself talk!" Jayden's eyebrows met his hairline.

"Yo, you do *not* need to get so angry," Jayden muttered.

"*I* don't need to get so angry? *I* don't? *You're* the one who has argued incessantly at me at nearly every game that I have had to suffer in with you just because you don't like me! I *loved* basketball. I still love basketball, but you made me *hate* the games in high school and again in college because you had to continue doing it and I had to keep officiating your stupid games! *I* don't need to get so angry? Maybe if *you* didn't get all in my face and make me scared all the time then maybe I would've dated other guys. But, I was *terrified* of other men. Because maybe they would end up having terrible anger issues and think that I'm stupid and that I don't know what I'm talking about like *you* have always made me feel!" I screamed. I had never seen Jayden look so shocked in his life.

"Yo, G, I'm sorry for arguing with you all the time. I didn't know that—"

"No! You don't know anything! You think Dr. Adler would've killed me? He *cares* about me. He's the only person who doesn't care what kind of person I am and, yet, sincerely cares about *me*. After all the torture that you've put me through in my life, *he* was the one who was there for me through all of it. He helped me and you think he *killed* me?"

"Grace, I—"

"*Stop fucking apologizing!!*" I yelled. I felt my face burn from anger as I tried to walk far away from Jayden. *I just want to leave*, I thought over and over.

But, over and over I kept reappearing in front of him. His face looking more broken each and every time. Finally, I just walked as far away as the ghostly string would let me. Collapsing onto the ground, I pulled my legs into my chest as I felt myself start to cry. Anxiety crusted over my lungs, like a slab of ice, making it harder and harder to breathe. I didn't *want* to have this conversation. I didn't *want* to talk about Dr. Adler.

"Grace, look at how you're reacting about me just talking about your therapist," Jayden said, walking closer to me. I glared up at him, the ghostly tears running down my face.

"Leave me alone, Jayden," I choked out.

"This is an irrational reaction and I know because I have irrational reactions on the court—"

"Oh my *God*, please leave me alone!" I yelled out. He stared at me, as if I had gone crazy, and then his face turned back into a statue, once again.

"Fine, Grace," he said, fed up with me. He was always fed up with me.

"Fine," I responded, defiant.

fifteen

THE FIRST TIME that Dr. Adler and I spoke about Jayden, in depth, was after my mother died. It was when Jayden made that comment about how my mom must be rolling around in her grave after the grade I just got.

"Why would he say that?" I had said, in between sobs.

"Boys say things to hurt others. That's just how they are," is how Dr. Adler responded.

"*You're* a boy," I accused him. He smiled slightly.

"I'm the exception," is all he said. Dr. Adler and I had started to have more in depth conversations about Jayden after that one session. What was his family like? How long had I known him? What did we usually talk about?

"Jayden and I fight about everything," I rolled my eyes as I said this. "Just today, we had an argument over whether peanut butter and jelly was a good sandwich or not. Who argues about peanut butter and jelly? It's a staple in most households."

"What was his argument?" Dr. Adler asked. I scoffed.

"He said that peanut butter and jelly sandwiches weren't good to those who were allergic," I muttered. "But, I'm sure there's people allergic to bread and cheese. So, for them, no sandwich is a good one."

"Who started this argument?" I paused to think.

"It was Jayden." Looking back, Jayden pretty much started every argument that we ever had. He would just come up to me every day, as if he were looking to fight with me. It would be over the most mundane things at times also. It was like he *had* to take the opposite take to every opinion that I ever had in life.

"Or would *you* always take the opposite opinion?" Dr. Adler had asked after I made this realization.

"I—*He's* the one who is always starting the argu-ment. How am I taking the opposite opinion if that was my opinion in the first place?" I had asked, fuming at the question.

"Well, from my understanding, it seems that you have a slight obsession with Jayden King," Dr. Adler had said, closing his notebook. He stared at me with his ice-gray eyes, his voice even as he accused me of this.

"Obsession?" I asked, shocked from the word. How was I obsessed with Jayden? I wasn't obsessed with him. He didn't fill my thoughts all the time. I would only just think about how angry I was over the stupid arguments that we had.

"In order to continue the conversation, you might take the opposite approach during these... 'arguments,'" Dr. Adler said, leaning forward in his chair. His eyes were studying me, but in a calm, calculated sort of way. I didn't necessarily *feel* judged, but I didn't like the feeling that it did give me.

"I'm not obsessed with Jayden," I said, pushing back on his analysis. He didn't look surprised that I said this.

"Grace," he said, calmly, as he looked through his notebook, "You have talked about Jayden for the entirety of the hour for the past few weeks. You've barely touched on your mother's death." I stared at him.

"But—" *Wasn't* he *asking me questions about Jayden?*

"I feel that maybe you have become fixated on Jayden in order to distract yourself from thinking about your mother," Dr. Adler said, leaning back in his chair. He wrote down something in his notebook.

"You think that?" I had asked quietly. He looked up, over his square-shaped reading glasses, and then nodded.

"I suggest," he said, taking off his glasses, "that you stop seeing and talking to Jayden King for the foreseeable future."

This was something he had insisted on. And coincidentally, Jayden and I had that huge argument where I thought that he let those boys in the locker room talk about me the way that they did. And I didn't speak to him for the rest of the school year, or even the beginning of the next one. Not until Will forced us together later on in senior year.

But, that argument with Jayden forced me to accept something that Dr. Adler would repeat to me a lot throughout the years: Boys just say things to hurt others. But, Dr. Elijah Adler was the exception.

* * *

"Are you seriously not going to talk to me?" Jayden asked as he was getting ready for bed. I turned away from him so that I didn't have to see his face. I couldn't leave his sight, that stupid, ghostly string was tying us together. And it wouldn't break no matter what I did. I tried again, grabbing the string that recently appeared and tried to rip it apart.

"Why do you keep doing that to the air?" Jayden asked. His voice sounded tired. I wasn't going to respond to him. He didn't deserve any response. The lights turned off and then I heard him get into his bed.

"Grace, seriously, I'm sorry for bringing up your therapist," he sighed. "I didn't know it was such a sore topic for you." I didn't say anything. It wasn't that I was angry at *him*. I didn't know *who* I was angry with or *what* I was feeling right now. There was silence for a moment longer, and then I heard him sigh and turn over in his bed. Soon enough, his breath became heavy and moments later, he was snoring. I turned around to look at him.

Once again, his eyebrows were scrunched together and it looked like he was really angry with someone. *Probably screaming at me about Dr. Adler*, I thought to myself. That's what it looked like anyways. I crawled into his bed and stared at him. His curly hair was covered up with a black durag, which somehow made his face look a bit angular. Jayden usually had soft features. A lot of curves were in his face, but with the disappearance of his hair, it made them look a bit more sharper.

I was never obsessed with Jayden, I thought to myself. Dr. Adler was wrong. But, as I stared into his sleeping face, I felt this overwhelming feeling start to bubble up in my lungs, making its way into every breath that I would take. I didn't know what to call this feeling, but it was almost suffocating me. Turning on my back, I tried to take a deep breath.

Even though I stopped talking to Jayden for a while, we still had basketball games where I was officiating and he was playing. Just like now, Jayden would yell at me for whatever foul I would call on him. It wasn't just me, I would remind myself. He would argue about every foul with every referee. But, it felt personal to me.

"You should stop officiating basketball," Dr. Adler suggested in one session. I stared at him, in disbelief.

"I can't stop officiating basketball. I love doing it," I argued.

"Don't you like playing basketball more than officiating?" he asked. I blinked.

"Yeah, I mean—yeah I like playing it," I said, dreading the direction this conversation was going in.

"So why are you officiating?" Dr. Adler asked. It was a simple question, but it felt bitter somehow.

"Because I want to—"

"You want to continue to be close to Jayden," Dr. Adler finished. I frowned at him.

"Dr. Adler, I don't officiate because of some boy," I said, slowly, feeling... I didn't know how I felt. Almost guilty in a way.

"Oh?" he simply said.

"No, I just want to be a part of the NBA someday. And I know I'm never going to be able to play basketball professionally, with my height, so officiating is the next best thing," I muttered. Dr. Adler stared at me, his eyes quietly studying me as they usually did.

"You should stop officiating and start playing. It will help you," he eventually said. And so, a few days later, I quit officiating. But, I didn't start playing either. It was too late to try out for the girl's basketball team and I was a senior anyways. So, what was the point?

When Jayden and I started talking again, I didn't mention it to Dr. Adler. I hadn't hung out with Will in so long because I didn't want to hear about—or even see—Jayden. And, I had this nagging feeling that if I told Dr. Adler, he would make me stop being friends with Will altogether. Not being friends with Will forever was a future that I couldn't imagine.

But not officiating was depressing me. I wouldn't want to leave the house or my bed. I wasn't motivated to do anything. Eventually, my dad talked to Dr. Adler, and I was granted permission to officiate once more. But, the season was already over by that point. So, I looked forward to doing it in college. Jayden wouldn't be there so there wouldn't be a problem doing it. Except, Jayden chose to go to the same school I went to, on a full ride basketball scholarship no less.

The sun was starting to rise as I tried to collect my feelings about Dr. Adler. I loved Dr. Adler, like one would love a father or a brother. But, thinking about it, I was also scared of Dr. Adler. And as I thought more about my life that was now lost, he controlled every aspect of it. Wouldn't he be the one to control whether I had the privilege to continue living or not? Would he be that sinister?

Jayden wriggled around uncomfortably as the sun started to hit his face as I stood over him. He was an annoying kid. He made my life so terrible. This is what I always told myself. But really, he was just someone who had authority issues, definitely some anger issues when he would play basketball, and liked to tease me for the most part. Were those qualities of his bad to the point where I hated him? Did I actually ever really hate him or was I being forced to?

My head was starting to hurt as I tried to think back on the moments that I had with Jayden. He was annoying, that was something I could agree with myself on. I thought he was obnoxious and argumentative. I thought he could be stupid. But, he wasn't boring. Every conversation I had with him was exciting, and something that I would think about for days on end.

His eyes opened, sleep still weighing them down. He didn't seem surprised that I was standing over him, even though I hoped that he'd scream in terror. Instead, a long arm came up and touched my face, softly, as if he couldn't believe that I was real. I stared at him, a feeling that I couldn't describe started to bubble up in my chest.

"Why did you choose to go to the same college as me? You had a ton of offers," I heard myself say.

"I wanted to stay with you," he whispered, and then his arm dropped as he fell back asleep. I stared at him, unblinking, as I processed what he said.

I didn't think I hated Jayden King. I don't think I ever truly hated him. Instead, I think I...

I shook my head. No, that's not possible. *No*, I forcefully thought to myself. That would be insane, but the thought kept burning its way through my mind, burning my tongue. It would be insane. I would be crazy. For the whole time I was living, only to realize after death, that I actually *liked* him this whole time?

sixteen

"WHY ARE you acting weird right now?" Jayden whispered to me in the middle of a game. I avoided his gaze. *I couldn't like him.*

"What do you mean?" I asked. He frowned at me as his coach called for him to pay attention. The ball was passed towards him and he ran down the court, my ghostly body being dragged with him. I realized I didn't need to walk or run alongside him during these games anymore. My ghost body would just float to wherever he was if I just let myself. It was an odd feeling, though. It was as if my legs were separating from me over and over again.

"I just did a foul and you're not yelling at me for it," Jayden muttered under his breath so only I could hear. I shrugged. I wasn't a referee anymore. I was dead. Plus, I wanted to limit all interactions with Jayden as much as physically possible. *It was impossible for me to like him.*

"I literally just traveled and you're not going to say anything?" Jayden asked, getting frustrated at my lack of conversation.

"I don't know what you want from me," I said, leaning back into the air. "It's not my job anymore." I completely avoided his gaze and I could see from my peripheral vision that he frowned at my lack of eye contact.

"What is going on with you?" he said, more to himself than to me. *I like you and I have no idea why*, I screamed in my head. Instead, I shrugged in response. The game continued, but it was clear that Jayden was having a bad night. He was missing shots that he usually did easily.

"Is everything okay with you, man?" Tre asked as he ran past him. Jayden waved him away, sweat pouring down his forehead. I peeked at him, trying hard to not let him see that I was doing so. The statue of Jayden King was back. The reason? Who knew but it was probably going to be blamed on me, once again.

The game ended with the Washington Wolves losing by a point. Jayden wiped the sweat off of his forehead with the back of his hand. He looked furious, and I tried to stay as far away as I possibly could.

"Were you talking to someone during the game?" Tre asked, as he walked up to Jayden. Jayden frowned as he chugged down his water.

"No," Jayden lied. Tre frowned at his response.

"It seemed like you were talking to someone next

to you..." Tre said slowly. Jayden stared at him, obviously trying to think of some excuse.

"Listen, man, the death of someone close to you is really hard to go through. I totally would understand if you were hallucinating her in the game there. I feel like that's normal since she was always calling you out and stuff," Tre said, putting a hand on Jayden's shoulder. Jayden stared at it, still wondering what he should say.

"I'm fine," Jayden said. "I'm not tripping, if that's what you think."

"No, no," Tre said, shaking his hand, "I don't think you're tripping. I think you're hallucinating." Jayden glared at him and Tre took his hand off of his shoulder.

"The team is just worried about you," Tre muttered. "Coach is, especially." Jayden looked back at Coach Jackson who quickly turned his head when he realized Jayden was looking at him.

"Did he ask you to talk to me?" Jayden asked, his voice monotone. Tre shrugged.

"We're all just concerned that you're taking this death really hard," Tre said. Before Jayden could respond, Coach Jackson walked up to him.

"Jayden, they want you on the podium after you shower," the coach said. He shared a meaningful look with Tre behind Jayden's back as he pushed Jayden forwards. Jayden slowly walked forwards and then stopped and stared at me, wide-eyed. This was the first game that Jayden was back for, and in the one practice that he had since my death, we successfully avoided the locker room. How were we going to avoid it now?

"Uh, actually," Jayden said, backing away from the locker room doors as we got closer and closer. "I think I'll just skip the shower and go straight to the podium."

"You don't want to shower?" Coach Jackson said, his face contorted into disgust. Tre's face echoed the coach's.

"Nope," Jayden said quickly. Then he examined their faces, "Yeah, I'm just trying this new thing of, like, letting the sweat soak into my skin."

"Say it's a new skincare trend," I said, going along with what he was saying.

"It's a new skincare trend," Jayden clarified. The coach and Tre just stared at Jayden's face, flabbergasted.

"A skincare trend," Coach Jackson said, in disbelief. Jayden nodded, obviously proud about the cover-up that we just did, but I was less sure.

"Are you seeing someone, Jay?" Tre asked slowly. Jayden shook his head.

"Nah," he said, "It's just good to take care of your skin, you know?"

"*Is* it good for your skin? Or will it just give you ringworm?" Tre said. Jayden laughed uncomfortably.

"Oh, you got jokes," Jayden said, clapping him on the shoulder. "Anyways, I'll just head to the podium now." And with that, Jayden swiftly turned around as I pushed him forward as fast as possible.

As we were leaving, I heard Coach Jackson ask Tre: "Did a white girl tell him that nonsense or something?" Jayden apparently heard it, too, because he chuckled at me as we walked away. His smile lit up his whole face and it was as if the sun had peeked out from behind the storm clouds. I couldn't help but stare at him. And when I realized that I stared a bit too long, due to the budding frown that was appearing on his face, I looked away quickly.

"We need to get you to the podium," I said, not making eye contact. I felt him stare at me for a second before continuing to walk.

"Seriously, what's going on with you?" he asked. I didn't respond. And luckily, I didn't need to because he was about to get up in front of a bunch of reporters in order to talk about the game. That's what they called the podium. It was a seat in front of a mic with a paper background that had logos and hashtags. And in front of that, were rows of reporters waiting with their cameras and their notepads. Jayden's eyes looked down as he sat in front of the mic, appropriately displaying the sadness after losing a game.

"Jayden," a reporter yelled out. The cameras flashed and it was hard for my eyes to adjust to it, "How did you feel about your performance in this game?"

"You know," Jayden said, leaning forward a bit, "I am disappointed with how I performed and I am just sorry towards my teammates for not doing better. But, I'm going to work on my shortcomings and hopefully bring a better performance next game." He then nodded to another reporter who had their hand up.

"The last time you played was a home game as well and you were ejected from the game. Do you think your anger issues keep you from focusing on the court?" This was a bit of an odd question. I could see Jayden's eyes glaze over.

"I didn't handle that game as well as I would have wanted to. I'm under a lot of stress, but that isn't any excuse. I apologized after that game for how I behaved and I am still sorry now. I am trying to get it under control," is how Jayden responded. He was more mature up in front of these reporters than I had ever seen him be in my life.

"In regards to the ref that got you ejected from the game," the same reporter continued. I watched as Jayden's frown deepened, "What was your relationship with her and will there be an investigation into whether there was bias during those games or not?" Jayden paused.

"What do you mean by bias?" he asked. I could see his blood start to boil.

"Well, the Wolves have won nearly every game that this referee officiated," the reporter clarified.

"We *lost*, last game," Jayden pointed out, his voice like ice. "And she ejected me from the game, rightfully so. She always called out my fouls, almost meticulously, so how would she have been throwing the game for me?" The mic was taken away from the reporter and I saw Jayden relax a little. The next reporter was handed the mic, and Jayden's gaze fixated on him like a predator about to kill.

"Did the referee's death cause you to be off your game tonight? There are rumors of you two dating, before her passing. What do you have to say to them?" Jayden was seething. I could nearly see the steam that was coming off of his body. Underneath the table, his hands folded into fists, his knuckles white.

"We weren't dating," he said, the vein along his jaw pulsating, "We hardly knew each other. We went to the same high school, the same college, and were into the same sport. But, all we ever did was argue."

"You say you barely knew each other, but you were the one who found her body," another reporter questioned. Jayden's eyes roamed the crowd for the reporter.

"Yes, I found her body," Jayden confirmed, "But, we weren't friends. We had mutual friends, but, personally, we weren't super close."

"What do you have to say about the rumors regarding her death?"

"What rumors?" Jayden asked, his face like stone.

"That she killed herself because of you bullying her on the court all the time," the reporter said, his face unmoved. Jayden stared at him, and I could almost see the knife that was thrown into his chest.

"Killed herself?" Jayden muttered. And then a little louder, "Grace wouldn't have killed herself. And not over me anyways."

"Could you clarify on that? If you two weren't

close, how would you know if she would or wouldn't have killed herself?" a reporter asked.

"It was confirmed in a press conference this evening that she struggled heavily with depression and anxiety, due to your behavior throughout her life, Mr. King. What do you have to say about that?" another reporter asked. Jayden stared at these reporters like he was a deer caught in the headlights.

"Could we please stick with basketball and the game?" he asked, but it was like his words were drowned out by the noise of the flashing cameras, the scribbling of the reporters, and their shrill, bird-like voices piping up.

"Let's go," I said, putting a hand on Jayden's shoulder. He looked up at me, his face morphing into that of a confused boy, and he got up off of the chair and walked out of the room. Closing the door behind him, he rested his head against the cool wall of the hallway.

"What are they talking about?" he asked. I waved my hands in front of his face, hoping that some air would be created from them to cool him down, but the air didn't move. I was still just a part of it.

"I don't know," I muttered.

"What press conference?" he asked me, his eyes desperately searching mine.

"I don't know," I repeated.

"Did I really make you depressed?" he asked me, after a long moment of silence. There was a silent question that followed after that: *Did you really kill yourself?* Before I could answer, the team's manager came running out of the door.

"Let's go, King," he said, putting a hand on Jayden's back. Jayden's eyes looked at me, reminding me of when he was a kid in Mrs. Viper's English class. But, I didn't know what to do or say to make him feel better. I barely understood what had just happened in that conference room.

"We're going to get a car sent for you and send you home, right away," the manager told Jayden. But Jayden's eyes were glossed over. They were almost like glass eyes. If he blinked, I was sure that they would shatter into a million pieces. I wasn't sure what was said that made him feel like this. I didn't know why he was so devastated.

"I wasn't depressed because of you. I was never depressed because of you," I said, softly, guessing at the cause of his anguish. But, I didn't know if my words even reached his ears.

seventeen

JAYDEN PLAYED the video over and over again on his phone as he watched from the couch of his living room. He hadn't moved for about an hour. The video was a press conference that was done by the police of Washington D.C.

"After looking over Ms. Lee's records, it is clear that she was diagnosed with depression and anxiety by her therapist. She was taking medication for it, and unfortunately, one night the wine that she drank reacted badly to her medication. It is unclear whether she purposefully took her own death or not, at this time, but it is highly probable," the police officer told the crowd.

"Did you know that the written records of her therapy sessions have been leaked online?" a reporter asked. When I first heard this, my body went numb. Everything that Dr. Adler had written down about me was out in the open, for anyone to read.

"We are investigating the leak currently and will punish the perpetrator accordingly," the officer responded.

"In those records, it is clear that the basketball player Jayden King was bullying her for a long time. Will he be questioned at all in regards to this?" another reporter asked.

"This tragic death of this young lady was either an accident or a suicide. We will not be taking any more questions at this time," the officer answered. Then the video ends. And Jayden replays the video over again.

"Jayden," I said, kicking his feet. He glanced up at me over the top of his phone.

"Am I imagining you?" he asked, his voice quiet. I had never seen him look so unsure of himself before.

"I don't feel imagined," I muttered.

"Did you kill yourself?" he asked, almost meekly, like he didn't really want to know the answer but needed to.

"No, I don't think so," I said, unsure of myself. *Did* I take my medication that day? I remembered telling Dr. Adler I took my anxiety medication that morning, though I wasn't sure if I actually took it or not, or if I even took any of my antidepressants that day. But, would drinking wine at the end of the night mess with my medication that I took that morning?

"Are you real?" he asked, almost desperately. His eyes gazed into mine, as if he were trying to drink in the essence of me. To feel that I was real.

"I *am* real," I said, trying to shake off his gaze. It was unnerving, him looking at me like I was... dead.

"You're a ghost though," Jayden said, to himself. He stared at his phone that was playing the same interview again. "I *must* be tripping."

"How would you know all those things about Will if I wasn't real?" I pointed out. "Those were only things I knew about him. Plus, I wouldn't ever kill myself. And I'm pretty sure I've had a glass of wine with my medication before." Jayden looked up at me, his eyes desperate for some kind of excuse as to why reality was telling him I killed myself while the ghost of me was telling him I was murdered.

"You have, right? You wouldn't kill yourself because of me, right?" he asked, grabbing my hands. I felt my face get hot from the touch. *Chill out, Grace*, I thought to myself. This is *not* the time to get worked up.

"Why would I kill myself because of you?" I fake laughed as I pulled my hands out from his grip. "I don't care what you think about me."

"Then, why did you cry about me so much in your therapy sessions?" he asked, switching to another tab on his phone and holding them up. *When did he even find those?* He blinked.

"I—Well, first of all, those notes are overly exaggerated. I didn't cry about you in my therapy sessions. It was one time where I cried about you and that was after my mom died and you made that super insensitive remark," I stammered.

"What did I say?" he asked, innocently. I stared at him in shock.

"You don't remember telling me that my mom was probably rolling in her grave over my exam grade?" I asked. He looked up to the ceiling as he thought to himself. Then, he pursed his lips and shook his head.

"No, I don't remember that," he said, going back onto his phone. "But, I'm sorry for saying it." I rolled my eyes. Obviously, he was doing a little better now.

"If you *are* real, and you didn't kill yourself, I think your therapist leaked these notes," Jayden said, "And forged them to make me look bad."

"Okay, well, he always thought you were terrible for me. So he probably over-exaggerated them in the moment anyways," I said.

"You're not defending him?" Jayden asked, an eyebrow raised. I sighed, loudly, avoiding his gaze once more.

"There's something that Dr. Adler has always kind of drilled into my head since I started seeing him, basically. He says, 'Boys say things to hurt others. But, I'm the exception.' This has always been brought up when I talked about another guy, no matter who the guy was or what they said. A guy asked me out? It must've been as a joke. They were making fun of me. Boys say things to hurt you. Only Dr. Adler is nice to you. A boy gave me a compli-ment? They must've meant it sarcastically. There must be something wrong with my hair or my eyes, because boys only say things to hurt me. Only Dr.

Adler wouldn't," I said, hugging myself as Jayden stared at me. His expression morphed from confused to angry.

"And I realized... he made it so that I didn't have any friends," I said slowly. "Girls were just as vicious as boys. They knew I was special and they would always hate me for it. I wasn't a part of this world. I was only meant to look at it," I shuddered as I remembered the words that Dr. Adler would say to me.

"I suddenly started to have a life, Jayden. I got into the NBA as a referee! My lifelong dream. I started talking to Valentina more. I reconnected with Will. And, Dr. Adler felt all of these things weren't good for me," I muttered.

"He was losing control of you," Jayden said, putting the pieces together. I nodded and then shrugged.

"I don't know. I feel conflicted about this. I just know he didn't like you. And it was drilled into me how terrible you were to me. And, you *were* terrible to me. But also, that was kind of our dynamic, wasn't it? Just us arguing about the stupidest things," I said. He looked at me, his eyes gazing into my left and then right eye as I watched the wheels in his head start to turn.

"You think he killed you," Jayden confirmed. I paused for a moment, and then I nodded slowly.

"I think he did. But, I don't know how the autopsy report was manipulated. I *know* I was poisoned. I feel it in my heart," I said. Jayden grabbed my hands once more, squeezing them until they started to throb a little.

"You're real, right?" he said. I winced as I pulled my hands from his grip once more.

"Yes, I'm real," I said.

"Okay," he said, nodding his head. "Then, I'm going to get that weird ass therapist into jail, and my reputation cleared."

"As a bully?" I asked. He nodded his head. I laughed.

"Jayden," I said, "Everyone already knows you're kind of a bully to the refs." He frowned as he thought about this.

"Okay, but I don't want people to think that you killed yourself because of me. It's disrespectful to you," he muttered. I looked up through my eyelashes at him as he went back to his phone. Since when was he so protective of me? Was he always and I just never noticed?

Jayden looked up at me, and gave me a weird look. I quickly ducked my head. *I need to stop staring at him*, I thought. It was weird. And—I glanced up at him for a moment before turning to look at the coffee table in front of me—I didn't want him to ever know that I liked him. I was dead. It just wouldn't be fair to either of us. *So*, I vowed, *Jayden can never know*.

eighteen

"I AM NOT GOING to sneak into a pathologist's office and try to find evidence that they lied on Grace's autopsy report," Will said, crossing his arms as he glared at both Jayden and I.

"You *have* to," Jayden insisted, "I can't do it!"

"And why ever not?" Will asked.

"Because my face is very easily recognizable. Plus, no one would question a white boy snooping around someone's office," Jayden pointed out. Will pursed his lips and then nodded at Jayden's logic. That wasn't something he could really argue with.

"Why do you even think the pathologist lied?" Will asked. Jayden and I exchanged a look.

The night before, I had Jayden snoop around to find out who was the pathologist that signed off on my autopsy. Autopsies were public record, especially after the police had closed a case. In the autopsy report, it was signed by a woman named Matilda

Herring. And, everyone has social media nowadays, even pathologists. There was hardly anyone in the world that was living in this time period that wasn't on Facebook. Even older folks were on Facebook these days. And what did I find while snooping on the web when I was nineteen? Elijah Adler's Facebook page.

So, all Jayden had to do was search for someone named Matilda Herring on Dr. Adler's mutual friend list, because he wasn't private for some reason, and we found her. Once we found her, we cross-checked her picture with a Matilda Herring on LinkedIn that was a pathologist in Washington D.C. It was the same woman. Not to brag, but Jayden and I were totally detectives in a parallel universe.

"It's the same woman," Jayden insisted as he went through all the steps to convince Will that the pathologist did indeed know my former therapist who probably killed me.

"I don't know," Will muttered as he switched apps to look at the woman in the Facebook picture to the woman in the LinkedIn picture.

"Will is practically face-blind when it comes to women," I muttered, throwing my hands up.

"I mean, they both have brown hair," Will said, shrugging.

"Are you for real? It's for sure the same face, Will," Jayden said, astounded. It was *literally* the same face.

"And both their names are Matilda Herring. I feel like that's not *that* common of a name," I pointed out.

Jayden nodded his head at me and then told Will what I said.

"She's right," Jayden responded, backing me up. Will gave a doubtful look towards Jayden, as he scrunched up his nose.

"Since when were you two on the same page about anything?" Will asked, but a small ghost of a smile appeared on his lips.

"Since you were apparently face-blind," I muttered.

"We can't let Grace's murderer walk away, free and unharmed," Jayden said, gripping Will's shoulders. He shook him a little as Will just stared up at the ceiling.

"Please illegally sneak into the pathologist's office and search for any evidence that she might've lied on the report in order to appease this Adler character," Jayden begged. Will sighed loudly as he took a step back. He stared at Jayden for a moment, and then stared at an empty space next to Jayden. Jayden cleared his throat.

"She's on the other side of me," he whispered. Will quickly looked over to where I was.

"Okay, I'll do it," he said. "But, if I go to jail, you can't go to the afterlife until after I'm a free man." I rolled my eyes at his request.

"Fine," I said. "It's a deal." He put his hand out, as if to shake my hand, but instead it went through my stomach.

"Dude, you're standing too close to her. Your arm just went through her," Jayden exclaimed, disgusted.

His eyes met with mine as if saying: *Can you believe this clown?* I laughed at his expression.

"Oh, sorry Grace," Will said, backing up a little. He tried sticking out his hand again and Jayden just lowered it.

"Just, don't," he said. Will slowly lowered his hand in disappointment.

* * *

"Will said he'll meet us outside the hospital tomorrow," Jayden said, looking at his text. I watched as another text popped up, before he clicked the side button that made the screen go black. The name was "Valentina." I felt my heart drop a little.

But, before I could stop myself, I heard the words tumble out of my mouth: "You text Valentina?" I shut my mouth as soon as the words came out. Jayden narrowed his eyes at me and shrugged.

"Yeah, is that a problem or something?" he asked.

"It's not a problem," I said, quickly. Maybe a little too quickly. He looked me up and down as he typed in the code to his apartment. The door opened and he walked inside, letting the door slam shut as I was walking through. *What a gentleman*, I thought to myself. I might've been a ghost, but it's still a weird feeling when objects go straight through you.

"Why do I feel like it's a problem for you? Because she's your friend or something?" he asked.

"I just didn't think Valentina was your type, that's all," I said. He raised an eyebrow.

"She's got curly hair, a cute smile, and a banging body. You didn't think she was my type?" Those were all qualities that I didn't have. I subconsciously looked at my straight black hair and then looked back up at Jayden. *Shit*, I thought to myself. From the look on his face, he noticed the inner comparison that I did. I started to nervously laugh.

"You're right. She's definitely someone who I think would've been your type," I said, nodding.

"You literally just said that you didn't think she was my type," Jayden said, an eyebrow raised as a teasing smile started to appear on his lips.

"You know," he said. I could feel the bile start to come up into my mouth, "It *kind of* sounds like... you're... jealous?"

"I'm not fucking jealous, Jayden," I groaned as I rolled my eyes at him.

"A little... *too* defensive, maybe?" he said.

"Please, shut up," I said as I turned around to hide my face that was starting to turn red. When did he become so perceptive? "I'm not jealous. I just didn't know that you and Valentina were talking." Jayden laughed and poured some cereal into a bowl. Sometimes, at night, Jayden would just snack on cereal, but without milk. I wasn't sure why, but it was just a snack that he seemed to love. Tonight, it was Cinnamon Toast Crunch.

"Yeah, we're just talking," he said, once his

laughter faded. He stared seriously into his bowl of cereal.

"I didn't think you were that serious when it comes to dating," I muttered. He squinted his eyes at me.

"I'm not," he said. Then, he shrugged, "I don't know."

"You're not over Mia?" I half asked but mostly assumed. He stared at me and then shrugged again as he brought his bowl of dry cereal to the living room.

"It's been a year," he merely said.

"But, you're not over her," I pointed out. He shrugged again and turned his head away. The conversation was done. Just like always, he wasn't going to talk about something that he didn't want to talk about. But, the question was eating away at me. It had been eating at me for days.

"What did she mean?" I asked, barely speaking. He frowned as he leaned towards me, slightly.

"What?" he asked.

"What did she mean? The other day. Mia, I mean," I said. His face had turned to stone once more.

"Grace, I don't really want to talk about this," he muttered. I felt my face burn from embarrassment. It wasn't what I was thinking. But, suddenly, it was as if I were watching myself say the words that came out of my mouth, unable to stop myself.

"Did you talk about me that much during your relationship that you made your girlfriend feel insecure?" *Why, Grace? Why would you say that?* I chastised myself. His eyebrows lowered towards his eyes and his jaw clenched slightly.

"I didn't talk about you that much," he said, sternly. "She just assumed things."

"Why did you care so much if I cut you out of my life or not?" I asked, almost trying to push him into the answer that I wanted him to say. Jayden turned his upper body towards me, and put the bowl of cereal on the coffee table.

"*Why* did you cut me out of your life, Grace? I understand the first time, but the second time? The third time? The fourth time?" I shifted uncomfortably on the couch, taken aback by his frustration.

"I mean—"

"The last time you cut me out, right before I started dating Mia, I just got recruited to be on an NBA team. I thought you of all people would be proud of me, and instead you stopped talking to me. You blocked me on everything," he said. There was something behind his eyes. Something in his stone-like expression that made my heart ache. But, I was embarrassed for cutting him off at that time, so I couldn't *really* tell him why.

"Dr. Adler told me to—"

"You never blocked me before, Grace. In all the times where you were 'mad' at me and didn't want to speak to me anymore, whether that was your decision or it was your therapist trying to get you to do it, you never blocked me, bro," he said, his eyes boring holes into my face.

"I was upset that you got into the NBA," I said, dejectedly. I was dead. Who needed embarrassment anyways?

"You were upset?"

"Because I know you, and we've known each other for a long time, you being in the NBA meant that I... probably wouldn't be able to officiate in the league," I muttered. "And, you knew that was my lifelong dream."

"You knew that being a professional basketball player was mine," he accused.

"Was it *really* your dream? Or did you just want to appease your dad?" I asked.

"Why would I want to appease my dad?" he said, crossing his arms.

"Jayden, you are always trying to impress your dad. That's why you didn't want me to be on your ass that night," I pointed out.

"I didn't care either way," he said, grumpily as he turned back to eat his dry cereal.

"Oh-kay, you *did* care, and please for the love of God, eat your cereal with milk," I cried out, gesturing to the bowl that he was holding close to his face as he inhaled Cinnamon Toast Crunch. He looked up at me in disbelief.

"Why would I eat it with milk?"

"You're supposed to eat cereal with milk," I insisted. He shook his head.

"There isn't any rule that cereal *must* be eaten with

milk. Besides, I'm not much of a milk drinker," he shrugged as he continued to eat his cereal.

"You don't have to drink the milk. You're just supposed to have the cereal soak in it," I said. He scrunched up his face at my words.

"That sounds disgusting," he muttered.

"Okay, maybe I didn't describe it well enough, but it's supposed to be in milk."

"Ah, I don't know," he said. "It sounds like it'll get all soggy."

"It's *supposed* to get soggy."

"Would you eat a soggy salad?" he asked, randomly.

"What?" I said, frustrated.

"Would you eat a soggy salad? It's a simple question, G," he said.

"No, I wouldn't eat a soggy salad, but—"

"Exactly," he said, talking over me.

"—cereal is not salad!" I finished. He shrugged.

"Crunchy cereal is better than soggy cereal," he said.

"Ask Will, right now," I ordered. He smiled slightly.

"Bet," he said. He took out his phone and texted Will. We waited in silence, our breath bated, until the text notification popped up on Jayden's phone.

"Stop arguing with each other. You're arguing with a ghost. People prefer different things," Jayden read the text like a robot. He looked up at me.

"I feel like this is a win for me," he said. I scoffed.

"I seriously don't know how you came to that conclusion," I said, rolling my eyes. He just slowly put a handful of dry cereal into his mouth, making eye contact with me the whole time, and then chewed it slowly.

"You're annoying," I muttered. He smiled a bit as he turned back towards the TV.

nineteen

OUTSIDE OF THE HOSPITAL, Jayden handed Will something that looked like a small ear plug in the car. Will stared at it as he held it gingerly with his pointer finger and thumb.

"What is this?" he asked.

"It's to put in your ear," Jayden said, pointing at his. Inside of his ear canal was one of the tiny ear plugs.

"Oh, spy gear?" Will said, pushing it into his ear. Jayden nodded, a goofy smile on his face. He was way too excited about this.

"Just so you know," I reminded him, "We're messing with a potential murderer. So let's not get *too* excited." Jayden put up his hands as he motioned for me to calm down.

"Chill, G," he said. "Today, we're only messing with his assistant. It'll be fine."

"Hopefully," I muttered. Jayden turned towards Will, who looked utterly confused.

"It's not fun being the only one left out of the conversation, guys," he said. "It's like listening in on a telephone conversation except you can't even hear the tone of the person on the other line."

"Why do you want to hear her tone?" Jayden asked.

"It would just be nice to hear her voice at all, to be honest," Will muttered. He coughed into his arm and then tried to change the subject.

"So, you'll be able to hear what is said through this little thing?" Will asked. Jayden nodded, the twinkle in his eye coming back.

"Yeah, I can hear you and you can hear me. We can talk out loud using these things. Cool, right?" Jayden said.

"Did it cost a lot?" Will asked. Jayden looked down at his phone. Another notification from Valentina. I felt my lips tighten into a line as I sat back in the car seat.

"Oh, just a bag," Jayden responded, as he put down his phone.

"Good thing I still have this doctor's coat from that one Halloween," Will muttered, smoothing out the collar of the coat.

"No one will question you," Jayden said, clapping a giant hand onto Will's narrow shoulders. "Just walk with confidence and everyone will think you belong."

Will nodded, taking a deep breath before getting out of the car.

"I'll let you know if I find anything," Will said.

"Remember, her name is Matilda Herring," I said. Jayden relayed the message for me and Will nodded in my general direction.

"I'll do my best," he said. Then, he closed the car door. I climbed over the console and sat down in the passenger seat that Will was just sitting in. Jayden and I both watched as Will awkwardly walked into the hospital.

"Goddamn it, I told him to walk with confidence," Jayden muttered.

"You know I can hear you, right?" Will's voice said through Jayden's ear plug. Jayden looked surprised, as if he forgot that he could hear him. I couldn't hear Will's voice all that well, but in the silence of the car, it wasn't too hard to make out the words that he said.

"Why won't Will date anyone?" I asked, after sitting in silence for a while. It was a question that I was curious about for years, and I felt like now was as good a time as any. Jayden looked at me, either surprised as to why I didn't know or why I was asking.

"Do you have a thing for..." Jayden remembered that Will could hear him, "a thing for him?" I laughed and waved the words away with my hand.

"No, no. I don't have a thing for Will. I've just always been curious about it. Lots of girls liked him in high school and probably in college, too," I said.

"Will, did girls like you in college?" Jayden asked.

"Please don't talk to me," Will responded. "This is nerve wracking enough." Jayden gave me a look and a sideways smile.

"I visited Will a couple of times in college. And there were girls in his friend group that definitely were feeling him," he said. Then he shrugged one broad shoulder of his. "But, Will's asexual so he doesn't want to date anyone."

"I can't believe you're outing me right now," Will's voice floated out through Jayden's ear.

"She was asking," Jayden responded, "And it's not *really* a secret, is it?"

"Why didn't he ever tell me?" I asked, more to myself than anything. But, Jayden felt the need to respond anyways.

"Well, I mean, you knew about him throwing up after kissing Shyla and then he never dated anyone again, so I don't really know how you didn't figure it out," Jayden pointed out.

"You didn't know about him throwing up after kissing Shyla, so how did you know?"

"He told me, 'I didn't have a great time kissing Shyla. It was awful.' So I asked him if he was gay. And he said, 'No, I think I might be asexual.' And that was it," Jayden explained, making his voice higher to mimic Will's.

"I have papers I have to give to a Dr. Herring," Will said, responding to someone we couldn't hear, "Thank you." The person we couldn't hear must've given him some kind of direction.

"Okay, my point is, he told you and he didn't tell *me*," I said.

"Well, maybe because you never asked," he said.

"Is she wondering why I never told her?" Will asked through the ear plug.

"Yes, and she seems really upset by it too for some reason." I heard Will sigh dramatically.

"I just didn't think I needed to tell her," he said. My jaw dropped at hearing these words.

"Am I, like, *not* your best friend? Why wouldn't I need to know?" I asked.

"Will, she's found out that *I'm* actually your best friend," Jayden laughed.

"It's not about being best friends or not. Jayden just asked if I was gay and I wasn't gay. You never asked anything so I just didn't feel like I had to tell you, or anyone for that matter," Will explained. "Also, I'm in her office."

"Oh my God," I muttered under my breath. Jayden and I waited, holding our breath for a moment.

"Wait, how did you even get in?" I asked. Jayden repeated my question.

"The door was unlocked," Will said. I could almost hear him shrugging.

"Lucky bastard," Jayden muttered under his breath and then said, "Check her computer first. There has to be some kind of correspondence between her and Dr. Adler." Will silently started to type on the computer. I watched as a notification appeared on Jayden's phone.

"Valentina?" I asked. *Again,* I silently finished my

thought. Jayden looked up from his phone, a slight smile on his face from reading whatever it is that she texted him.

"Yeah," he answered, and then went back to writing out his response to her. I tried to swallow down the pang in my chest as I leaned forward a little, curiosity eating away at me. He moved his phone out of my view.

"What are you doing?" he asked.

"What are you guys talking about?" I said, propping my head up with my hands. He stared at me weirdly.

"Are you okay?" he asked.

"I'm fine," I lied. "I was just curious about what you two were talking about." He looked me up and down and then leaned back into his chair, relaxing once more.

"We might go on a date," he said. I felt my eyebrows jump up.

"What?" I asked, not completely surprised. "She's a ref though. I'm sure it's against the rules."

"Yeah…" Jayden said slowly, "I might be taking a leave of absence from the league." My eyebrows stayed high on my forehead. *Well, that was surprising.*

"What do you mean?" I asked. "You love being in the NBA." *And you're really great at basketball*, I almost said but stopped myself. *Complimenting* him? Did I *want* to have a giant sign on my forehead that read: I'm in love with you?

"Yeah, I love it, but," Jayden said, shrugging a little,

"There's a lot of backlash about your death. And about the possibility that I bullied you so much that you killed yourself." His eyes refused to meet mine.

"Oh," I said.

"I just don't really want to see the comments anymore," he muttered.

"But, you'll see them even if you take a leave of absence," I pointed out. He shrugged.

"Probably not as much," he said under his breath.

"Jayden," I said, "We're going to clear your name." Jayden stared at the steering wheel, his eyes not moving. He thought for a long time, until finally he looked over at me.

"But, what if we don't find anything?" Jayden whispered, his voice low. As if on cue, Will piped up.

"I think I found something," he said. Jayden's eyes widened with excitement. How quickly he went from utter sadness to unbridled joy. He was very much like a kid, sometimes. I couldn't help but smile to myself.

"What did you find?" Jayden asked. Paper being rustled was heard through Jayden's earpiece.

"I found this piece of paper. It looks like a diagram of a body and I'm pretty sure it's Grace's autopsy," Will said.

"What makes you sure?" Jayden said.

"Well, and I can barely read this handwriting, but up on the top, it says Grace. So, I'm assuming that's Grace Lee," Will pointed out. Jayden rolled his eyes at Will's response.

"But, I don't know if this will be helpful at all,"

Will added, as we heard him flip the paper over. "There's just a lot of writing describing her body. Not really anything about possibly being poisoned."

"Damn," Jayden mumbled to himself.

"It does say 'possible overdose' with a question mark on it. So, they did think it had something to do with medication," Will said. Then we heard Will rummage through something.

"Though," Will said, "the toxicology report would be what would determine the cause of death. They said it was her antidepressants or anxiety meds, so that should show up in the toxicology report."

"How do you know this?" Jayden asked.

"I watch a lot of crime shows," Will muttered. He then went "Aha!" as the sound of paper rustling came through the ear plug.

"What did you find?" I asked as Jayden repeated the question.

"The toxicology report," Will almost sang. Before Jayden could ask what was on it, the sound of a knock interrupted our excitement. I looked through the car window, and I could feel the air leave my lungs at the sight. His knuckles were resting on the window, as a sinister smile separated his lips. He adjusted his glasses before motioning for Jayden to lower his window. If I had any blood left in my body, it would've run cold. I would recognize those gray eyes anywhere.

"Dr. Adler," I breathed, and Jayden glanced slightly back at me. He rolled down the window and leaned out of the car slightly to address him.

"Yes?" Jayden asked.

"I saw you from across the parking lot," Dr. Adler said, his voice that consistent even tone of his. "You're Jayden King, the basketball player, correct?" I could see Jayden's hands ball up into a fist, his knuckles almost white.

"Yes, that's me. Are you a fan or something?" Jayden said, smiling slightly. He was hiding his disgust pretty well.

"My fiancée and I are *huge* fans," Dr. Adler said. "Would you mind if you sign my card?" *Fiancée?* My dead heart started to race.

"Sure, do you got a pen?" Jayden asked. Dr. Adler clicked a pen in his hand and handed it over. Jayden signed the business card, which clearly read "Dr. Elijah Adler, Therapist" on it.

"What are you doing at this hospital, if you don't mind me asking?" Dr. Adler said, straightening up so that he wasn't hunching over through the window anymore.

"My friend needed to get picked up," Jayden lied. Dr. Adler's eyes were unmoving.

"I see," he said. He put a hand over Jayden's open car window as he leaned down once more.

"You were friends with Grace, weren't you?" he asked. Jayden stared at Dr. Adler, his jaw muscle twitching.

"It's as if she's still here with us, isn't it?" he almost whispered, his voice dropping slightly. I saw Jayden frown and then watched as Dr. Adler glanced over to where I was, his eyes flashing with slight, but swift, anger.

"Be careful," he warned Jayden. "You don't want anyone to think that you've gone crazy." And I could swear he looked straight at me.

"HE CAN SEE ME," I whispered after Dr. Adler left. Jayden glanced over at me incredulously as Will was saying that he was coming back to the car with the evidence.

"What do you mean he can see you?" Jayden asked. I looked over at him, almost desperately.

"He can *see* me. He looked straight at me!" I exclaimed. He looked taken aback at my tone of voice, having never seen me this terrified before, and put up his hands.

"Hey, it's okay," he said, letting his hands fall onto mine. I looked at them, focusing on the veins that were raised and visible on the back of his hand. His long brown fingers gripped the edges of my small ones.

"Calm down, it's okay," he said. It was then that I realized that I had started to hyperventilate. His brown eyes looked deeply into mine and it was as if the world stopped around me. My breath held itself in my chest, not daring to be let out.

"Okay, breathe out," he said, demonstrating a slow breath. I breathed out, slowly, in conjunction with him.

"How do you know Adler looked at you?" Jayden asked quietly, calmly.

"Usually, their eyes can't focus on me," I heard my voice say. It sounded like a child's, "but his eyes focused on *me*. On *my* face."

"Okay," Jayden said, leaning back in his chair. His hands left mine and rested onto his lap. The air felt colder around my hands, somehow. My hands craved the heat of his.

"So, he can see you as a ghost, who cares? I mean, *I* can see you as a ghost," Jayden pointed out. "It's not a big deal." I leaned away from him.

"It's not a big deal," I repeated. Just as I was starting to calm down, the car door opened.

"I got it," Will said, his eyes and face exhilarated. He then proceeded to sit down on me, his body going through my ghostly one. Jayden's eyes almost fell out of his face.

"WILL!" he cried out. Will panicked, almost dropping the papers that he had in his hands.

"What? What?" he frantically asked.

"You just SAT on her!" Jayden said, gesturing towards Will and I. Will stared at him for a moment and then got up quickly out of the passenger seat.

"Oh my God, Grace," Will said, panicking. "Are you

okay? I didn't see you there." I tried not to laugh at his obvious joke.

"I'm fine. You just went through me," I said, getting up to go into the backseat. Jayden's eyes followed me, which indicated to Will that I was out of the passenger seat. Will sat back down.

"Will!" Jayden exclaimed, in the same tone. Will quickly jumped out of the seat.

"Is she still there?" Will asked, panicking. Jayden chuckled to himself.

"Nah, I'm just playing. She's in the backseat now," Jayden said, causing Will to grumble to himself about how Jayden jokes around too much as he sat back down.

* * *

"You're still going on this date?" I asked, as I looked over the toxicology report that was on Jayden's dresser. He left it there so I could read over it as he got dressed.

"I'm not going to stand her up," Jayden said.

"The report says I had snake venom in my system. Snake venom!" I repeated. Jayden popped his head out of his walk-in closet, his shoulders and collarbone were bare. I averted my eyes immediately, heat rising to my cheeks.

"We already knew you were poisoned," Jayden pointed out.

"Yeah, but shouldn't we take this to the police?" I asked.

"And make *me* their prime subject? No, we need evidence it was Adler. Then we can take it to the police," Jayden said, his voice slightly muffled.

"Are you really going to go on this date?" I asked, walking closer to the closet. Jayden walked out, dressed in a nice blue sweater and black slacks.

"What do you think?" he asked, spinning around as if he were about to break dance. He looked beautiful. I felt my face blush.

"Great," I muttered, ducking my head. If he noticed, he didn't say anything and he immediately walked into the bathroom to check his hair.

"I'm going on this date because I think she's cool," Jayden said, answering my earlier question. I stared at him in the mirror, trying to desperately get him to not go on this date with Valentina.

"You just found out that your friend was *actually* murdered and that you're not crazy. Don't you need to, like, I don't know, process that?" I asked, my voice almost frantic. An eyebrow raised on his face as he looked at me through the mirror.

"I've been knowing you were murdered, Grace. It isn't news to me," Jayden said.

"Well, what about Mia?" I asked, crossing my arms. Jayden's eyes steeled.

"What *about* her?" he asked, his voice monotone.

"You still are in love with her," I pointed out. Jayden almost laughed at my claim.

"I'm not in love with Mia," he said. He looked like he wanted to say more, but he didn't.

"What about your career?" I asked. Jayden sighed as he turned around to look at me.

"Listen, I know she's your friend and all, and it's weird to you, but I'm going on this date," he said. I looked at him, searching his eyes for something, anything. A sign that showed that he was joking, but there was nothing in his eyes to reassure me. It felt like he was ripping my heart out.

"If you go on this date, I'm going to make you look insane," I threatened without thinking, desperation clouding me. Jayden frowned at me.

"You wouldn't," he said.

"I would," I insisted. Jayden threw up his hands as he walked out of the bathroom.

"Why are you so upset about me going on a date with Valentina?" he asked. I put my hands on my hips as I looked away from him.

"Like you said, I don't want you to go on a date with my friend," I lied.

"You're dead, Grace. You can't control what your friend does," he said, exasperatedly.

"I don't care," I muttered, childishly. "If you go on a date with her, I will haunt you forever."

"It seems like you're already haunting me forever," he said under his breath.

"I will haunt you even after I cross or whatever happens after we find the murderer," I warned.

"Grace," he said.

"Jayden," I used his same tone. He sighed dramatically.

"I'm going on this date. I'm going to live my life and stop obsessing over your murder and death," he said. "And if you make me look crazy, I will never speak to you again."

"Well, if you go on this date, I'm going to make you look crazy, so…"

"So? So? Whatever, Grace. Do whatever you want," he said, walking out the bedroom door. I tried to plant my feet firmly on the ground, but the ghostly string pulled me forward.

"Fine!" I exclaimed. "I'll just make you look crazy to her then!"

"Fine," he said, not looking back at me. "Psycho motherf—"

"I can *hear* you!" I yelled at him, trying desperately to not be dragged along.

"Can you stop dragging your feet? I feel like I have a thousand pounds attached to me," Jayden said, moving forward as if someone was pulling him back. I pulled on the string more.

"I'm not even a thousand pounds," I said, almost satisfied that he can feel the string, too. Even if he couldn't see it. He turned around quickly.

"Grace," he said, his puppy brown eyes pleading with me, "Please." I let go of the string, and he straightened up. He stared at my hands and then looked back up at my face, but he didn't say a word.

"I just need to move on, Grace," he said, his voice

thick. *Yeah*, I thought, feeling myself shatter into a thousand pieces. I was dead. He needed to stop mourning that death. And I was just a constant painful reminder that someone close to him, whether we were friends or not, was murdered.

"I need to move on," he repeated, his eyes not meeting mine as he turned back around to walk out the door. I heard the unspoken words that hung in the air. He needed to move on from me.

twenty-one

I TRIED to pick up a french fry that was in the red and white carton on the diner table. Jayden's eyes were unblinking as he tried to not look at my attempt.

"I just wish I could eat one," I groaned as I tried to pick one up again. The veins in Jayden's forehead were popping out from concentration.

"Are you okay?" Valentina asked as she grabbed the french fry I was trying to eat. I groaned in protest. Jayden plastered a smile on his face.

"Yup, perfectly okay," he said, a hint of falseness in his voice. Valentina giggled a little.

"Okay, because your eyes are bulging out," she teased. He smiled, without showing any teeth as his eyes darted to me and then back to her.

"I used to say you had bug eyes all the time," I muttered, trying to eat another one of her french fries. I lowered my head to the sticky table as I groaned.

"I can't believe that Grace would do that to herself,

can you?" Valentina sighed, brushing a perfect ringlet from her face.

"If you believe that I killed myself, Valentina, why would you go on a date with my supposed bully?" I asked, gesturing towards Jayden. Jayden stayed silent as he tried very hard not to look at me.

"Nah," Jayden muttered, "She doesn't seem like the kind of person who would kill themselves." Valentina's eyes widened at the easy way that Jayden referred to my suicide.

"I don't believe you bullied her into it, though," she reassured him, as if she heard my earlier question. Obviously, she thought I killed myself.

"Yeah? You're the only one, it seems like," Jayden said.

"I know you didn't, because you cared so much when she passed. I mean, you even thought she was murdered," she said. He looked like he wanted to say something to her in response, but instead he lowered his hood over his face more as the waitress came to ask them if they needed anything.

"We're good," Valentina said, smiling, tapping Jayden's hand. I felt like someone had just punched me in the chest.

"Honestly," I muttered, giving up on my mission to eat a french fry, "What do you guys even have in common?" He curled his fingers underneath his hand and then put it under the table as he glared at me for a moment. Then he focused his gaze on Valentina.

"So, have you always loved basketball?" he asked.

The conversation was drier than the Sahara Desert. That's for sure. Valentina shrugged a shoulder as she dipped a french fry into a glob of ketchup.

"My family was always into basketball. I have a huge family, mostly brothers. And they taught me how to play and everything. I was on the basketball team in high school, but didn't cut it for college. So, I decided to officiate," she said.

"Oh, Grace was never on the basketball team in high school," Jayden answered. "She was always officiating." Valentina's eyes were downcast, as she stared at her half-eaten meal. She then smiled brilliantly at Jayden.

"Do you think we could not talk about Grace?" she asked, slowly and carefully. Almost as if she were walking on glass. Jayden seemed taken aback by that.

"Sorry, was I talking about her too much?" he asked, almost embarrassed.

"Yeah," I said, laughing. "You were." After every single thing that Valentina would say, he would find some way to relate it back to me. It was amusing, and it made my dead heart beat a little quicker. Even though I knew it was probably just because I was sitting right in front of him, next to his date.

"Not too much," Valentina said, shaking her head. "I get it. She just died a couple of weeks ago. It's hard to go through something like that."

"Something like what?" Jayden absentmindedly said.

"Well, she was a close friend of yours, wasn't she?" Valentina asked, gauging his response.

"I mean," Jayden laughed a little to himself, his eyes catching mine, "I don't think she'd describe me like that."

"I guess technically by everyone else's terms," I said.

"Yeah, I guess technically," Jayden responded, laughing. He stopped suddenly as he realized he responded to me out loud. Valentina stared at him for a long while.

"Are you doing okay?" she asked, looking through her long eyelashes.

"Yeah," Jayden responded, staring at his food as he lied, "I'm completely fine."

* * *

"Seriously, what is *wrong* with you?" Jayden exploded once we were back in the confines of his apartment.

"Whatever do you mean," I muttered, trying to look innocent but failing miserably.

"Grace, why would you do that to me?" he asked, putting his head into his hands and then letting them slowly peel off of his face, making his face look like it was melting.

"I didn't do anything," I said. Which was kind of true. I didn't *really* do anything. Did I try to make the lights flicker? Yes, but the lights wouldn't move. Even when I tried to use the light switch, it still wouldn't turn off because I couldn't touch it. I couldn't make anything float. I couldn't even possess Valentina. As a ghost, I was pathetic.

"You were distracting me the whole time and I just don't understand why you were doing it," he said, throwing himself onto the couch. He turned on TLC in order to watch some kind of strange reality show.

"I told you I didn't want you to date my friend," I pointed out.

"Why do you even care, though?" he said, his eyes not even looking at me.

"It's just because she's my friend," I lied. "Plus, I don't even see how you guys have anything in common besides me."

"Besides you," he repeated to himself. "Why did you make me talk about you the whole time?"

"I didn't," I said. "That was all you."

"You were distracting me the entire date, so that's why I was talking about you," he said, more to himself than to me.

"It's just awkward," I said, quietly, "Me being there."

"Well, it's awkward for me *too*. That's why I asked you to hide in the booth behind me," he replied.

"Why do you want to date her anyways?" I asked, without thinking.

"Because she's pretty, why else?" he said.

"Does nothing else really matter to you, Jayden?" I asked. He finally looked over at me, his expression unreadable.

"What is going on with you, honestly, Grace?" he asked. His eyes narrowed as he stared at me in confusion, as if he were trying to figure out some difficult puzzle.

"Nothing is going on," I said, a little too quickly. "I just don't understand how you can go on a date with someone you don't even have a connection with."

"Is this about Valentina or is this about me?" he asked, his words cutting through the air. I stared at him for a moment, feeling my cheeks burn.

"This is about Valentina," I said.

"Then, why does it feel like I'm cheating on you and you're pissed about it?" he asked. That was another thing about Jayden that was so infuriating. He always was bluntly honest.

"I don't know why you would feel like that," I muttered.

"*Yeah*," he said, pointedly, before turning back to the TV, "I don't know why you're *acting* like that." I stayed silent as I stared at him for a moment. Before I turned towards the TV to watch whatever reality show he was watching tonight, he pointed the remote at me.

"Why *are* you acting so childish about this?" he asked, his eyes boring into my soul. I scoffed.

"I am not acting—"

"You are," he said. "You were complaining the whole time, I could barely hear her speak, and you were moving around like you couldn't stand still."

"I wasn—"

"*Why* are you acting like this, Grace?" he asked.

"You hate me. You've always hated me, so why are you acting like you... you..." His face contorted into confusion once more as he stared at me, hard.

"Of course I hate you," I lied, not letting him finish that thought. I got up from the couch as he looked at me for a moment, hurt.

"I know," he muttered.

"I've always hated you," I said, convincing myself more than anything. "You were always picking fights with me, you took my best friend, you were always yelling at me on the court."

"Yeah, I get it, Grace," he said, his jaw clenched. He stood up so that I wasn't looking down at him. "I'm the guy who made your life, and now your afterlife, a living hell."

"Why do you always have to remind me that I'm dead?" I asked, quietly.

"Why do you care if I went on a date with Valentina or not?"

"Are you planning on making her your girlfriend or something?" I asked, indignant, as I crossed my arms across my chest.

"*Why do you care*, Grace? Just answer the question," he said, taking a step closer to me. I stared up at him, my eyes flashing.

"I don't," I lied. "You'll just throw away your career."

"Since when did you care about my career?" he asked, his voice low. "Since when did you care at all?"

"I *don't* care," I said, my voice quieter than I

wanted it to be. He stared at me, his face inches away from mine.

"You're dead, Grace," he almost whispered.

"Why do you keep reminding me of that?" I asked.

"To remind myself," he said. His dark eyes looked fearful for a second, then he took my face into his large hands and closed the distance between him and I. It was as though my blood turned into liquid fire.

twenty-two

IF I WAS ALIVE, I would've called Will immediately. This was something that I had to tell *someone* about. And I always got the best advice from Will. But, I wasn't alive. And I had no way of contacting Will.

I touched my lips, the place where he and I connected, and stared up at the ceiling made dark blue by the night. Jayden and I didn't speak after that one kiss. I had frozen up like a man who had been caught by Medusa's tendrils, while Jayden avoided my gaze and face after seeing my shocked response.

If I were able to talk to Will, I wasn't even sure what I would say. The phrase "Jayden kissed me" sounded like a foreign language. It wasn't something that was even thought of in the past. Well, except by Shyla.

I wondered if Will would've said he knew all along that this would've happened between Jayden and I. If he would've said, "I've known since the moment you laid eyes on him."

The first time I truly met Jayden was on the living room floor of Will's childhood home. He was sitting there, playing Crash Team Racing with Will, his tongue slightly out of his mouth as he concentrated on winning the race. I remembered being filled with unbridled hatred as I watched him yell out in excitement at him winning. It was the first time where I realized that if Jayden was around, I was invisible. He absorbed all the light around him until he was the brightest thing in the room, you couldn't help but look at him.

How cruel the universe was, I couldn't help but think. My whole life I felt invisible next to Jayden King, and now I was truly invisible to all but him. Perhaps even in life it was like this. I was invisible to everyone, except Jayden King. I felt my face flush at the foolish thought. That was just wishful thinking.

"What are you thinking about?" his voice startled me as I turned over to look at him. His eyes were low, still full of sleep, and he yawned as if to confirm my thoughts.

"Nothing," I said, quickly.

"You were thinking about Will," he said, knowingly. *When was he able to read my thoughts?*

"How—"

"I'll tell him, for you," he said, also knowing what it is that I wanted to talk about. I felt my face turn red.

"It's embarrassing, having you tell him," I muttered. He smiled, half asleep.

"I'm going to tell him anyway," he said. "He's my best friend, too." His hand touched my cheek, like the other night. Caressing it with his thumb.

"The night that you got ejected, how did your dad take it?" I asked the burning question that had been on my mind since that night. Jayden stared at me for a moment, waking up slightly. His hand dropped from my cheek and the cool air hitting it almost gave me goosebumps.

"Not well," he said, his eyes glazed over from the memory. "He asked something along the lines of when was I going to get my shit together. He also remarked about how the quality of players in the NBA has gone down since he was in the league."

"I'm sorry," I muttered. His eyes glanced over at me, and his whole face softened.

"It's not your fault," he said. "I'm sorry I made it seem that way." He touched my face again, the night making him more vulnerable. I leaned into his hand knowing that this was wrong, what we were doing was wrong. Every part of me screamed his name, but there was a gnawing feeling in the back of mind that told me that this was against nature.

He leaned forward and softly kissed my lips again, silencing that part of my mind. How did I go through my whole life not knowing how Jayden King tasted?

* * *

It was weird, the energy between Jayden and I the next day. It was as if we were trying to avoid talking about what had happened the night before.

"Do you want any cereal?" Jayden asked, awkwardly pushing the Cap'n Crunch box towards me. I simply stared at him.

"Oh right," he said to himself as he remembered that I couldn't eat. Yup, the energy between us was *definitely* weird. I had a feeling that even though Jayden was the one who initiated whatever it was last night, he wasn't going to be the first to start talking about it.

"Are we going to talk about—" Jayden's phone started vibrating. He stared at me, as if trying to ignore the call, but when he realized that I wasn't going to continue my sentence, he picked it up.

"Yeah?" he said. A high pitched voice came through the speaker.

"When were you going to tell me... I can't believe that you would do something so..." were all I could pick up from the ramblings. It was Mia. I could tell from her voice. I felt my face fall.

"Mia, what are you—"

"I'm here," I could hear that much. "So you better open your door." A knock came from Jayden's apartment door. It wasn't like how it was when Mia was banging on his door before. This was a much gentler knock. It sounded a lot like how... Jayden opened the door and standing next to Mia was Will. He brushed his wavy, blonde hair back out of his face.

"What is going on?" Jayden asked as Mia pushed her way into the apartment. Will followed sheepishly behind.

"I asked him that exact same question," Mia said, hands on her hips. She was still devastatingly beautiful, even though it was clear that she had just come from a workout. "Tell me why he responded that you think that Grace was murdered and are now trying to put her therapist in jail?" Jayden quickly shot a glare at Will, who cowered from his gaze.

"She literally was holding me by the ear," Will said, "I couldn't *not* tell her."

"It's none of your business, Mia," Jayden said, crossing his arms as he looked down at her. She pointed a finger up at him, taking a step closer. He took a small step back, which caused confusion to appear in her eyes. She put the finger that she was putting in his face behind her back.

"That girl is dead, Jayden. She went and killed herself and I'm *sorry* that happened, truly I am, and I'm sorry that you're going through this right now, but... you need to move on," she said. A sentiment that Jayden felt as well. He put his tongue against his cheek as he looked past her.

"She didn't kill herself, Mia. She's not that type of person," he said. Mia's face softened.

"I get it, Jayden. I understand," she said, softly. "It's hard to think that someone you cared about might've been feeling that much pain, but you *have* to come to grips that she's gone." She placed a hand on

Jayden's forearm, and he pulled away. Again, her face held so much confusion on it that it hurt me to even look at her.

"I'm still here," I said, quietly, in response to her words. Jayden's eyes glanced over at me and then looked back at her.

"She was murdered, Mia. You can look at the toxicology report. It says that she had snake venom in her system when she died. Not antidepressants," Jayden said, gruffly.

"I tried to tell her that," Will piped up.

"Snake venom, antidepressants—what's the difference? It's just something else that she killed herself with," Mia said.

"The difference is that they *lied* on her report. And that pathologist is Adler's fiancée," Jayden said. I could hear him start to get angry, just thinking about it.

"Who's Adler?" Mia asked, leaning back in her stance.

"Grace's therapist," Will said. "He *has* always been a little weird with her." His hand was on his chin once more as he thought.

"Jayden, wake up!" Mia said, clapping her hands in front of his face. "Her therapist *murdered* her?"

"Yes, Mia, he—" She held up her hand.

"I don't care if he murdered her or not. It's dangerous for you to get involved. *If* he murdered her, he could easily kill you as well for sticking your nose in it," Mia said. "Or worse."

"What's worse than dying?" Will asked. Mia turned to look at him.

"Prison," she simply said.

"I'm not going to stop going after him, Mia," Jayden said, saying her name with a level of intimacy that he and I had never reached, will never reach.

"Why? Why can't you stop, Jayden?" she asked, her eyes desperately begging him to discontinue his search for justice. Jayden looked away, unable to look into her eyes as he said his next words.

"You know why," he said. She stared at him, and I could see her heart breaking into a thousand tiny pieces. It was all over her face. She sucked her teeth and then spun around quickly, opening the door and leaving Jayden's apartment in a fiery flash.

"Why do you do that?" Will asked, as he stared at the empty space that Mia had just occupied.

"Do what?" Jayden asked, walking towards me so that he could be by my side. I looked up at him, and I could see how broken he felt.

"You love her," Will said, pointedly.

"Yeah," Jayden admitted, which created a pain in my chest that I didn't know I could feel, "But, you know I've always loved Grace." Will didn't look surprised by this revelation at all.

twenty-three

"WHEN DID THIS HAPPEN?" Will asked, his arms crossed over his chest as he paced back and forth in front of us. He had Jayden and I sit on the couch, with a pillow in my ghostly body so Will knew where I was exactly.

"Last night," Jayden muttered.

"I thought you went on a date last night," Will accused. Jayden shrugged.

"Yeah, I *did*, but then one thing led to another and I kissed her," he said. *At least we were talking about it now*, I thought to myself.

"You just got up and randomly kissed her?" Will asked. "She's a ghost."

"Yeah," Jayden said, resting forward onto his thighs, "It's weird. For some reason I can touch her and she can touch me. But, she can't touch anything else."

"Wow, interesting bit of information," Will said,

sarcastically. "I'm talking about how reckless you both are being. Mostly you, Grace." Will directed his gaze towards the pillow that marked where I was. I felt myself cower from his gaze. He was right. I *was* being reckless.

"Do you not understand the pain that he is going to go through once you cross over? And if you never go into the afterlife, and you're a ghost forever that he has to see, how is he going to move on? *He's* alive, Grace. *You're* not. He has a whole future and life to live," Will lectured. I lowered my eyes, staring at the coffee table that was pushed behind Will.

"It's not like she was the one who kissed me," Jayden said, defending me. "I'm the one who—"

"But she must've said something that hinted to how she really felt," Will interrupted, knowingly. He knew me all too well.

"She didn't say anything," Jayden muttered. "It was... more what she *didn't* say."

"You knew this man was in love with you the moment his twelve-year-old self saw you saunter into that sixth grade English classroom, and you choose after you *died* to let him have his chance?" Will accused me. I felt my blood freeze as I stared up at him in shock. Jayden was in love with me? The whole time I was living? Will's eyes didn't meet mine, as he wasn't able to see me, but I could see the anger that was brewing for his friend.

"I didn't know," I whispered. Jayden gritted his teeth as he turned to face Will.

"It's not her fault. It's mine," Jayden said. "I was the one who kissed her. I was the one who never told her. And I'm going to be the one who will have to deal with my feelings when the time comes." He took a deep breath before glancing over at me. But, my eyes were still on Will, who glared at me with a look I had never seen grace his delicate features before.

"This is wrong, Grace. And you know it," he said. And every part of me agreed with him.

* * *

I was pissed. After that argument, or more a one-sided argument, with Will, I was angrier than I had ever been. Or perhaps being a ghost just made me feel my feelings more intensely. Either way, I was mad at myself for letting Jayden kiss me, twice, and was mad at Will for being completely correct. It was wrong. It was *wrong* to have Jayden attach himself to me when it would ruin his life. But, Will's words were harsh. I understood that Jayden had a whole life to live, but mine was unfairly cut short. Wasn't there a bit of sympathy for me who had their first kiss after their untimely death?

I glared at Jayden as he ran up and down the court. Why did he even decide to kiss me? If he was really in love with me since laying his eyes on me, as Will claimed, why didn't he ever act on it? Would I have thought it was a joke and slapped him across the face?

Probably. But, he never actually *tried*. Why was this all on me?

"Charging," I said as Jayden rammed into a player as he was trying to get to the basket. He shot the ball anyways, but missed. The referee at the game called the same foul as I did.

"Please, Grace," Jayden said, his eyes flashing at me. I shrugged off his slight anger. He clenched his jaw and then turned back to playing the game.

"Defensive foul," I said, next to Jayden, as he grabbed the other player in order to keep the player from passing by him. It was subtle though. I doubted I'd be able to see it if I weren't standing right next to him.

"Shut *up*, Grace," Jayden said through his clenched jaw.

"The fuck you just say to me?" the player said in response as he swiveled around Jayden and scored a point. Jayden sucked his cheeks into his mouth as he glared at me. I continued to call every foul that I saw Jayden do as the game progressed. And if he didn't make a foul, I just told him what he was doing wrong in general. He did his best to ignore me, but again, it wasn't his best game. Fortunately, the Wolves still won.

Jayden avoided the reporters after the game and ducked out of the roaring stadium after the win, his coach still calling from behind him. When he was sure no one could hear us, he turned to me, grabbing my arm.

"What is wrong with you?" he hissed, a phrase I had started to get used to. I shrugged, my eyes flashing as I glared up at him.

"I'm just doing my job," I said.

"You're dead," he whispered. "Your job is done. And you're distracting me from mine. I thought you cared about my career." His eyes looked a little hurt before they turned into that statue that I would see time and time again. I felt my anger start to melt away. I was always using it as a defense mechanism.

"I'm sorry," I whispered. He stared at me for a moment longer, as if trying to figure out what my deal was.

"Is this because of Will?" he asked. "Are you mad at me because of Will?"

"I'm mad at you because of *you*, Jayden," I muttered.

"Yeah, but it's because of what Will said, right?" he asked. Before I could answer, a voice came from behind him.

"Who are you talking to?" Tre asked, staring at Jayden like he had gone insane. Jayden let go of my arm, but it must've looked like he was holding onto air. My heart beat quickly as I stared at Tre. He was going to think Jayden was crazy.

"No one," Jayden said quickly, turning around to face Tre. Tre stared at him, concern marring his brows.

"I heard about Grace," Tre said. "My grandma had really bad hallucinations after my grandpa died, so I get it."

"I'm not having hallucina—wait, what about Grace?" Jayden asked. Surprise filled Tre's face.

"Oh, you didn't hear?" Tre asked. He rubbed his forearm as he spoke, "I was trying to keep tabs on the news about her, since we all care about you and all. They were going to give back her body to her family since the autopsy is done and everything. But, it's been stolen."

"What?" Jayden asked, his eyes widening.

"Yeah, I thought maybe that's why you were doing so badly—"

"Tell the coach I need to go home. I need a break," Jayden said, walking into the locker room.

"Where are you going?" Tre asked.

"Back to D.C.," Jayden responded.

* * *

Jayden continuously kept reading the various articles that were giving updates about my case as we waited in the airport for our flight. The only reason why my death was even in articles in the first place was because they were linking every little thing to him. My mental health records were leaked, so Jayden had a bad game. My body was stolen, so Jayden obviously wasn't doing great.

They called for us to start boarding, and Jayden held his carry-on bag with one hand while still reading on his phone in the other.

"How in the world did they lose a fucking body?"

he said, out loud, forgetting that there were others around us. People just stared at him as he showed his boarding ticket. We were riding in first class. It wasn't my first time in first class. He rode in first class to all his games, and lately, I was forcibly brought along. But, it was the first time that it was just the two of us. He sat down in a seat that had walls surrounding it for privacy. I just stood in the little cubicle-looking thing with him.

"I just don't get how they lost your body," he muttered. I stared at him intensely.

"Jayden, you can't talk to me on a plane," I whispered. "There's other people around and they'll think you've gone insane."

"I don't care if people think I've gone insane, Grace," he whispered back. "Someone stole your body, on the day that your family was going to take it, and they seriously don't think you were murdered?"

"Maybe they'll open up the case," I muttered.

"You know who took it, don't you?" he said as the video about plane safety started to play.

"We don't know who—" Jayden gave me a look that made me stop talking. We both knew who would take my body, who had access to my dead corpse.

"It was Adler," Jayden said. "I'm sure of it."

twenty-four

I STARED up at the glass office building. I, then, looked at Jayden in horror as he grabbed my hand excitedly. His touch electrified every nerve in my ghostly body. But, my absolute fear for his life brought me back to reality.

"You can't be serious," I said. He had driven into Arlington, Virginia in order to find my therapist's office, the address that he somehow memorized when he was signing Dr. Adler's business card.

"Deadly," he said, flashing me a smile as he headed into the office building, me in tow. That ghostly string that held Jayden and I together was starting to fray and I couldn't help the bubble of panic that was rising in my throat.

"Do you have a plan?" I asked as we took the elevator up to Dr. Adler's floor. Jayden shrugged, not looking at me.

"A vague one," he said.

"Did you tell Will your plan?" I asked. "Please tell me that you told Will where you'd be." Jayden gave me a knowing look and then sent a text message which showed Jayden's location.

"I'm going to be fine," he said. "He'd be stupid to kill a public figure in broad daylight." I chewed on the inside of my cheek as the elevator doors ding-ed open. Jayden confidently strolled up to the front desk and gave his name. They gave him some forms for him to fill out and sign, and Jayden slumped into his seat as he started answering all of the questions.

"He's going to recognize you," I hissed.

"I hope he does," Jayden barely breathed. "That's the point." I wondered when he even made this appointment. I was with him every day, all hours of the day, and never once did I see him on the phone with Dr. Adler's practice. Unless... I stared at his phone that he was twirling in his large hand—he made the appointment online and I never noticed.

"This is a dumb idea," I said. He ignored me, turning in his papers and smiling brilliantly at the lady at the front desk. I swear she blushed even though she was twice his age.

"No," I said, "This is the stupidest, reckless idea that you've ever had."

"He wouldn't kill me at his place of work," Jayden whispered, his breath tickling my ear. I chewed on my lip some more as we waited for his name to be called.

"Jayden King?" the worker said and Jayden raised a hand as he got up.

"Don't eat or drink anything he might give you," I said as we walked down the hallway towards Dr. Adler's office. This walk was familiar to me, even the smell brought back memories. Jayden gave me a nod, acknowledging that he heard what I said, and then walked into Dr. Adler's office. I watched as the string continued to fray. Worried, I followed in step with him.

"Mr. King," Dr. Adler said, getting up to shake Jayden's hand. Jayden shook it, eyeing Dr. Adler as he did. He just looked at Jayden with studious gray eyes, roving over him, and then towards me. Jayden noticed the action and stiffened slightly before they let go of each other's hands.

"Please, sit," Dr. Adler said, gesturing towards the couch that sat across his all too familiar armchair. Jayden sat down, facing Dr. Adler. Even sitting down, Jayden looked larger than my therapist. He was all limbs and lean muscle, while Dr. Adler was a skinny man. He wasn't short, but he wasn't necessarily tall either. Just average.

Dr. Adler adjusted his glasses as he looked over the information that was given to him from Jayden's forms.

"So, you're having trouble with the grieving process, are you?" he asked, his voice strictly professional. He looked over his square glasses, the same way that he did when he felt like I was wrong. I felt my foot start to tap, and I thought I saw his eyes dart to glance at it. I wasn't the only one who thought so as I felt Jayden shift his body on the couch.

"Yeah, my friend Grace died. You might know her? You said it was as if she were still here," Jayden said, getting to the point. *God, I wish he wouldn't do that*, I thought to myself. It didn't work the other two times; I didn't know why he possibly thought it would work this time.

"I did," Dr. Adler said, a small smile on his lips. He was amused. Amused that Jayden would try to confront him.

"For me, it feels like she's with me all the time. At all hours. Like, I'm being haunted by her memory or something," Jayden said, acting pretty well. He *did* take a theater class in college, just to mess with me since I was also in that class. I recalled that he was pretty good at it, like he was with everything he ever seemed to do.

Dr. Adler wrote down what Jayden was saying, as if he were really trying to do a session with him. I frowned at the gesture, knowing that all he wrote were lies about me.

"So it feels like she's physically with you, at all times," Dr. Adler said, looking up at Jayden. Jayden nodded.

"I mean, even now," Jayden gestured to me, "I feel like I can see her." Dr. Adler took off his glasses as he leaned forward, staring at me, and then back at Jayden.

"Sometimes, grief can cause us to have hallucinations. Especially if that grief is marred with guilt," he explained. Jayden nodded, appeasing Dr. Adler.

"Does this apparition of Grace's ever say anything?" Dr. Adler asked. Jayden pretended to think, and then he nodded slowly.

"Yeah, she keeps telling me that she was poisoned. Every day, all day she begs me to right her death so that she can go to the afterlife," Jayden said. "It's honestly been driving me crazy and it's been messing with my games." Dr. Adler wrote some stuff down, his gray eyes looking positively more alive than I had ever seen them.

"So she can't leave until you bring justice to her wrongful death," Dr. Adler said. Jayden snapped his fingers.

"Exactly," he said. Then, he started to cough. A lot.

"Are you okay?" I couldn't help but blurt out, watching as Dr. Adler's eyes focused on me.

He repeated my words: "Are you okay, Mr. King?"

"Water," Jayden choked out. "Please, I need some water." Dr. Adler reached for the bottle of water that was near his chair and Jayden shook his hand at it.

"No, I can only drink Evian," he choked out, before another fitful of coughs. Dr. Adler frowned, his calm mask dissipating.

"Wait here," he said as he exited the room. Jayden's eyes followed Dr. Adler out as he kept fitfully coughing until he felt that he was out of earshot. Jayden then stood up and quickly walked over to his desk.

"He can see me," I said.

"I realize that," Jayden said. The string between us was getting weaker, I could tell. He rummaged through Dr. Adler's desk.

"What are you doing?" I asked.

"I'm looking for an address," he said.

"To what?" I asked, nervous. He then pulled out Dr. Adler's phone and waved it in front of me.

"To his house," he said. He then opened Dr. Adler's phone—apparently people over thirty didn't have passwords, or maybe it was just Dr. Adler—and went through his GPS app. There was Dr. Adler's most recent address, and upon looking at the street view, it was definitely his home. Jayden took a picture of the address with his phone, exited out of the app, and then put the phone back into Dr. Adler's desk just as we heard his footsteps coming back.

"C'mon," he whispered to me as we quickly sat on the couch together. I heard the string start to groan and I couldn't help but start to stare at it in panic. Why was it starting to come apart? Why was my connection with Jayden starting to fade when our connection was just beginning?

Dr. Adler walked into the room and glanced at what I was looking at. The string, he could see the string as well. I saw the corners of his mouth turn up slightly as he handed Jayden the Evian water. Jayden coughed some more before hitting his chest, sticking to his story to the end.

"Actually, I'm good," Jayden said, putting down the water without drinking it. "Just a little cough."

"Interesting," Dr. Adler muttered.

"Well, I have to go. I have practice soon," Jayden said, moving to stand up. I stood up with him and as we turned to leave, I heard an audible snap. The string that held Jayden and I together, was now in the hands of Dr. Adler. He pulled me towards him, the string dragging me towards his side as I stared at him in horror. Jayden looked positively angry. He started forward as Dr. Adler started to cluck his tongue.

"Hallucinations are pretty serious, Jayden," he said, wrapping the ghostly string around his hand. The string that Jayden couldn't see. The broken part that still was around him seemed to almost reach out, wanting to connect with its other half.

"Let her go," Jayden said. He knew that there was something binding me to Dr. Adler, even if he could not see it for himself.

"You don't want to end up in a mental hospital, do you?" Dr. Adler asked, his voice even and calm. I could almost hear the smirk in his voice. Jayden stared at him in anger and horror.

"You would send me to a mental hospital?" he barely asked.

"It seems you think I'm holding Grace captive. Her soul," Dr. Adler said, "But, no one is here."

"You know that's not true," Jayden said, through gritted teeth.

"Perhaps," Dr. Adler shrugged, "But, no one can

see her but you and I, it seems. And I have the right to detain you, with my... *professional* opinion." I had never heard the word "professional" sound so deadly before and I could feel my heart hammering in my chest. Jayden stiffened.

"Just go," I said, quickly. He wouldn't be any help to me if he was locked up in a mental hospital. "I'll be fine." I smiled, repeating the mantra I used my whole life, but it didn't quite reach my eyes. I knew he would find me and somehow help me. His eyes stared desperately into mine, almost begging me to ask him to help me. And then he steeled his gaze, glowering at Dr. Adler.

"You won't get away with what you did to her," Jayden almost growled.

"We'll see about that," Dr. Adler said, pulling me closer to him.

twenty-five

"STOP RESISTING, GRACE," Dr. Adler grunted as he pulled me into his house. I spat on his face in response. He bound the rope tighter around his palm so that I was closer to him. Nowhere to run. I pulled on the string that was connected to me, hoping that I could somehow get away. I was a ghost. If there was nothing tying me to this monster, I would be able to float away as fast as possible.

"Now both parts of you are with me, forever," Dr. Adler said as he closed the door to his house. Both parts? I scrunched my face up in disgust. He *did* steal my body. Jayden was right.

Dr. Adler dragged me around the house as he put his belongings down, eventually gesturing for me to sit down on the rocking chair in his living room. He wrapped the rope tight around my midriff, tying me to the chair.

"Why did you do this to me?" I asked, my breath

catching in my throat. He stared at me, his even gray eyes studying me, even in this moment.

"When I first saw you, I knew you were mine, even though you resisted constantly," he said this crazy notion as if it were the most normal thing in the world.

"Why kill me then?" I asked. His head cocked to the side.

"You had stopped listening to me," he merely answered. So, that was the reason. I had become uncontrollable. Elijah Adler sat on the couch that was next to the rocking chair, typing on his computer.

"Why poison me?" I asked. "Why not just stab me? It seems you would've been happier doing that." Elijah laughed. His laugh disturbed me, as I had never seen much emotion emit from him before. He was always a constant calming presence. Now, he terrified me.

"I was going to take your body, after you had passed," Elijah answered, matter-of-factly. "But, your... friend found you before I could."

"You would've stabbed my body afterwards," I muttered. Elijah cocked his head to the side, still not looking at me as he wrote on his computer.

"No," he said, "Just kept." Chills ran down my spine. He was still calm, like he always was. But, instead of calming me, it made my skin crawl.

"Girls are always harder to control once they're closer to twenty-five," he said, giving out that information even though no one had asked. "You started to have your own mind. I couldn't let that happen. Not again." *Again?* I stared at him, the realization sinking in that I wasn't his first victim. Not by far.

"How can you see me?" I asked. Elijah laughed again. His laughter was hollow.

"Did you think only your precious Jayden could see you? Because of a soul connection?"

"I thought he had killed me... Before," I muttered. Elijah glanced at me, his eyes looking over his computer screen.

"I guess you weren't too far gone yet," he said, as if to himself. My eyes looked into his gray ones as I started to put the pieces together.

"You wanted me to hate Jayden," I said, almost accusingly. Elijah smirked and then shrugged slightly.

"You didn't need him in your life," he said. "I contemplated killing him. But, I thought his death would be more noticeable than yours. You didn't have many people in your life." *Because of you,* I wanted to shout out.

"I trusted you," I said, my words twisted in my mouth. He closed his laptop and stood up, his face inches away from mine as he leaned forward.

"If you trusted me, you would've done as I said," he said. "Why go back to officiating? I told you not to."

"I just liked to—"

"You were in love with that basketball player and would've done anything to stay close to him," he interrupted, making his own conclusions. "You were *mine*, Grace. Not his." His hand reached out to touch my hair. I flinched as he came closer, but his hand went through it. He couldn't touch me. I felt shocked as I looked up at him, while he looked downright furious. *He could touch the string, but he couldn't touch me*, I thought to myself. I stared defiantly into his eyes.

"I guess I'm not yours like you thought," I said. A rage that I had never seen before filled his face as he grabbed the ghostly string and dragged me up the stairs of his house. I tried not to move, tried to feel like I was a thousand pounds so it was harder for him to take me, but he still managed to get me upstairs. He opened up a secret compartment in the hallway of his house, and pushed me inside. It was the size of a closet and I saw the horrific sight of my body, laying propped up on the ground. Despite being carefully preserved, it had started to rot and the stench filled my nostrils almost immediately.

Elijah wrapped the ghostly string to a bar that was attached to the wall. That same bar held up my rotting human hands that were attached by handcuffs.

"You will stay here until you allow me to touch your soul," he ordered. His tone wasn't angry, but rather it was still as calm as ever. It disturbed me to my very core.

"What are you talking about?" but he closed the secret door anyway. The only light that emitted was through the outline of the door. I tried not to think about how my body was sitting right next to me. It was frightening, seeing my body without life animating it. It didn't even *look* like me.

I couldn't help but have fear creep into my chest

for Jayden. He was going to try to come here, I knew it in my heart. He wouldn't just leave me here. But him coming here... Elijah Adler had killed before me. He had even considered killing Jayden just to get him out of my life. If Jayden proved too much of a nuisance, he would kill him without hesitation. It wouldn't matter if Jayden was in the public eye or not.

Distantly, I heard the front door close and a voice echo throughout the house. A woman's voice. His fiancée, Matilda Herring. I started to shout, as loud as I possibly could. I knew she wouldn't be able to hear it. No one seemed to be able to hear me but Elijah and Jayden. But, I wasn't screaming for her to find me and free me. She wouldn't have done that anyways. For all I knew, she helped Elijah with everything. No, I didn't want her to hear me. Instead, I wanted to drive Elijah crazy. If he wanted me to be *"his,"* I would show him what a life of eternity with me would look like.

I screamed for as long as I could. I didn't have the same limitations as I would have if I were human. I was dead, and I was embracing it wholeheartedly. Unlike living humans, I had no need for sleep, no need for air. I could scream continuously until my soul disappeared. But, my soul didn't seem to realize that I was not quite human anymore. It gasped for breath that it didn't need as I screamed and screamed. I wanted to make him go insane. I wanted him to open the door. And I wasn't going to stop screaming, no matter how much my soul tried to stop me, until it was opened and I was free.

After what felt like hours, the door finally opened, and standing there was an incredibly pissed off Elijah.

"Stop it," he said, grabbing the string from the bar and dragging me towards him. I put my feet out as I tried to stop moving towards him, but he still pulled me near, his face close to mine.

"Scream again and I'll gut your boyfriend like a fish," he said, his eerily calm voice sending waves of terror throughout my ghostly body. His gray eyes stared deeply into mine as I held my chin high.

"You wouldn't be able to get close to him," I said. Elijah smirked as he brought out from behind his back the blue sweater that Jayden was wearing the night he kissed me. My eyes locked onto it, my body unable to breathe.

"I already know where to find him," he said. He then tied me back to the bar as I sat there, limp. He was in Jayden's apartment. Somehow, he was able to get into his apartment without us knowing. A horrific thought went through my mind as I stared into those cold, lifeless eyes. Jayden was going to die if he tried to come for me. The door shut, and I was in darkness once again.

twenty-six

I DIDN'T KNOW if there was anything that I could do. I was stuck in this makeshift room in the walls of a hallway the size of a tiny closet next to my rotting corpse. I tugged on the string that bound me to the metal bar that was attached to the wall. I didn't understand why I couldn't untie it. It should've been easy for me to. It was just a string. But, even when it was bound to Jayden, I wasn't able to break it or mess with it either. There must be some kind of reason that I couldn't manipulate it while Elijah could.

The growing light peeking through the outline of the secret door illuminated the room slightly so I could see my rotting self. I stared at it. Someone had closed my eyes, thankfully. I remembered the gray film that had started to overtake my usually bright, dark brown eyes. Looking away from my corpse, I shuddered. I thought being tied to Jayden was bad? *This* truly was hell.

I heard a murmuring of voices coming towards me and then fading as the seriously disturbed couple walked down the stairs. The door slammed shut, indicating that Elijah had gone to work. I breathed out a sigh of relief. At least, I didn't have to see him.

Then, suddenly, the secret door opened, allowing light to blind me as I blinked up at the shadow standing there. As my eyes adjusted, I felt my heart stop.

"Jayden," I breathed as every part of me started to sing his name. Jayden. Jayden. Jayden.

"What is going on? Can't you go through walls?" he asked, his smile teasing me. He bent down, onto his knees, as he put my face into his hands. His large eyes held so much concern over me, I felt like crying at the outpouring of love that was written all over his face.

"I'm fine," I said, but this time—for the first time —it wasn't a lie. His hands fluttered over me as he looked for any damage.

"I'm okay. He can't physically touch me, like you can," I said.

"I missed these eyes," he barely uttered. "They're my favorite feature of yours." My too small eyes. The ones that I hated. A surge of emotion filled me.

I wanted to keep Jayden's eyes on me. I didn't want him to glance over at my dead body propped up next to me. But, as I tried to move so that my corpse would be out of his view, his eyes glanced over at it. At me. And I saw the life drain from his eyes as he breathed in the smell of rotten flesh. Immediately, he turned around and emptied the contents of his stomach in the middle of the hallway. Grabbing his phone, he snapped a quick picture of my corpse handcuffed to the metal bar. He held his shirt over his nose as he grabbed my hand.

"C'mon," he said, pulling at my hand. But, the ghostly string was still attached to the metal bar.

"I can't move," I said. Confusion filled his face.

"What do you mean you can't move? You're just sitting here," he said. Then his eyes widened as he looked around the edges of the secret closet room. "Dude, is there some kind of spell trapping you in here?"

"No, you idiot," I said, rubbing my temples. "There's no such thing as magic."

"You can't blame me for believing, G," he said, "You *are* a ghost."

"I *know*," I grumbled. Then, I pointed at the string that was attached to the metal bar.

"This is what's keeping me from moving. It's attached to this," I said, touching the bar. Jayden squinted his eyes as he tried to look at what I was pointing at.

"I don't see anything," he said. I felt defeated as I sighed. How was he supposed to get me out of here if he couldn't even see the string?

"It's a string," I said. "It came undone when we were at his office. That's how he was able to grab it," I said.

"What came undone?" he asked.

"The string," I repeated.

"What string?" he asked. I groaned as I grabbed the string and shook it, even though he couldn't see it.

"*This* string. The string that was connecting me to you. The other half is still attached to you," I said, pointing at the string around his hips. It was reaching out, as if it wanted my part of the string to be attached once again.

"Oh, so that's what you've been holding onto sometimes," he said, mostly to himself. He looked at me as he thought.

"Just put the string in my hands, and I'll pull it off of the metal thing," he said, holding out his hand. His big, brown eyes looked up at me through his unfairly thick eyelashes as he spoke. I felt my body relax at his gaze. *Everything is going to be okay*, I thought to myself. Perhaps in vain.

I put the string in his hands and he wrapped his long fingers around it. From his face, I could see that he couldn't feel it either, but he gripped it as best as he could. He started to pull, the string quickly coming undone from the metal bar. My heart started to beat quicker in my chest. *We needed to go, we needed to leave*; every part of my body was screaming at me. Jayden grabbed my arm so that we could go, as I watched the string attach itself to Jayden's other half.

"He can *touch* you?" a calm, but angry, voice said from behind us. I looked over my shoulder and there, standing over Jayden, was Elijah Adler. His reading glasses slipped slightly down his nose, and his eyes flashed with an anger I hadn't seen in them before. I glanced down at what was in his hands and felt my eyes widen.

"Dr. Adler, *please*," I barely had time to say before he hit Jayden over the head with a golf club. Jayden immediately fell to the floor, his body limp. I stared at him, fear encircling me. I didn't realize I was holding my breath until I could see the rise and fall in Jayden's upper body. I breathed out a sigh of relief.

"He can touch you," Elijah said, fury dripping through every word. I felt myself start to shake as I turned my whole body towards him.

"Please, Dr. Adler. Don't kill him," I begged, "I'll convince him to leave. Please." Elijah stared at me, as he ran a hand through his slightly unkempt hair. His eyes were dead. I knew there was no hope for Jayden.

"I don't want to kill him, Grace. I really don't. But, he has left me with no choice," Elijah said, his mouth twisted in disgust as he looked at Jayden's body.

"I need to think," Elijah said, his voice uncharacteristically frustrated. He pushed Jayden's body into the secret closet, squishing him up against my corpse. And then he closed the door. I rushed towards Jayden's head as I tried to sit him up. Luckily, I could touch him and I pressed against the back of his head. Blood.

"Jayden," I said, shaking him. He needed to wake up.

"Jayden!" I cried out a little louder. He groaned a

little at hearing my words. *Oh, thank God*, I thought to myself. Looking around, I tried to figure out what could get Jayden to wake up completely. My eyes focused on my corpse as an idea came to the forefront of my mind.

I grabbed Jayden's head and pushed his body with my knees closer to the part of me that was rotting the quickest. Ironically, it was my chest. I pressed Jayden's nose towards my corpse's middle, letting him breathe in the foul scent. His eyes fluttered open as he gasped for breath, backing away from my corpse.

"What the fuck?" he said, more to himself than anything. He grabbed my hand as he looked at me.

"Oh my God, you're okay," I whispered, not wanting Elijah to hear me, as I untangled my hand from his and threw my arms around his neck. I hugged him close enough to breathe in his scent. He smelled sweet with a mixture of laundry detergent.

"I'm so sorry," I said as I started to cry. "I'm sorry, Jayden. I'm so sorry." He pulled away from my embrace as he looked at my face in the dim light.

"Hey, hey," he said, wiping my tears with his thumb, "It's okay, Grace. I'm fine. I'm okay."

"You're not okay," my voice caught in my throat, "He's going to kill you."

"It's okay," he said. He smiled slyly, a smile that I used to think I hated but actually secretly loved. He pointed to his left ear. My tears stopped as quickly as they had come as my eyes widened.

"No," I said. He nodded his head, as if he did something he should be incredibly proud of.

"Will is in here," he said, pointing to the ear plug. "And I'm sure he's called the police to Adler's house by now."

"I did," I heard Will's voice somberly say. I couldn't hide the joy that took over my face.

"I'm *so* glad you didn't decide to be an idiot today," I smiled. Jayden rolled his eyes.

"I've been a genius my whole life, G. Put some respect on my name," Jayden whispered. He moved to run his hands through my hair, but I flinched at the movement, remembering how Elijah tried to touch me. His eyes looked furious as he realized why I moved away, but then they were replaced quickly by a look of sadness. He balled his fingers into a fist and moved it away from my hair.

"I'll kill him," he said. "For what he did to you."

"Don't," I said. "He'll get what's coming for him."

"I also have his threat against Jayden recorded, so he's definitely going to jail. If not for your murder, at least for that," Will said over the earpiece. Jayden turned his attention to the closet door, his hands leaving me. This was the first moment that I had to process how close he was to me, and even in this moment, I could feel myself blushing.

"Okay," Jayden said, pushing against the closet door.

"He's going to come back to kill you. Once he decides how to do it," I said.

"Well," Jayden said, smirking at me, "We can't let that happen, now can we?" *Obviously*, I wanted to say. But instead I just rolled my eyes. I looked at the back of his head as he was lightly pushing against the door. His curly dark hair was matted with blood and I wasn't sure that he had stopped bleeding yet.

"Here's the game plan," he said, after he finished inspecting the door. "I'm pretty sure I can push this open. Once we get out, we can't leave. Not until the police come." I looked at him like he was crazy.

"You want to wait until the police get here? He could kill you in that time," I hissed.

"Grace, he has your body right *here*. This is all the evidence that the police need—plus the toxicology report that I sent in—to arrest him for your murder. I can't let him get away with what he did to you, G. I can't," he insisted.

"If you die, I'll never forgive you," I said, pointing a finger at him. He smiled, almost sadly.

"If I die, I'll get to be with you forever," he muttered. I stared at him, anger infesting my blood.

"Jayden, if this is a death wish—"

"It's not, Grace. I was just saying," he said as he pushed open the door. I stared at him, carefully studying his facial expression. Maybe it wasn't a death wish, but I knew if he did die, he wouldn't be that upset about it. I walked through it just as Jayden managed to break it open. That door was not made to keep a muscular person in. Before we got any further, I faced Jayden and stared up at him.

"Jayden, I'm serious. If you die, I'll never forgive myself. Ever," I said. My eyes stared deeply into his, trying to get the message across. He closed his eyes and then nodded before opening them again.

"Let's go find Adler," he said, smiling. But, I could see the worry that was quickly filling his eyes.

twenty-seven

IT DIDN'T TAKE LONG for Elijah to find us. And in his hand, he was holding a large kitchen knife. His gray eyes glanced at the string that was holding Jayden and I together and then darted up to Jayden's face. For someone who looked like he was about to murder someone, his demeanor was unnervingly calm.

"Trying to escape?" Elijah asked, his voice nonchalant. Jayden shrugged a shoulder, matching the tone of Elijah's, even though I could feel the hand in mine start to slightly shake.

"What? You thought the best course of action was by stabbing me?" Jayden asked, forcing a relaxed laugh to escape his lips. I knew there was no way in hell that Jayden was about to show that he was scared. Elijah's eyes glanced at our hands interlocked and then looked back up at Jayden.

"It's what I could do on short notice," Elijah said,

his voice sending chills down my spine. I tried to let go of Jayden's hand, in hopes that it would quell Elijah's growing murderous rage, but Jayden just held on tighter.

"Aw," Jayden feigned sadness, "No snake venom today? That *was* a pretty clever way to kill Grace, I have to admit." Elijah cocked his head to the side.

"I knew when that report went missing that it was you who took it," Elijah responded.

"Matilda Herring helped you, right? Why would she help someone like you?" Jayden asked.

"A lot of questions," he merely said. Jayden shrugged as he took a step back.

"It doesn't seem like I'll survive this encounter. Might as well get some answers before I die," Jayden said. Elijah seemed to weigh the pros and cons of answering Jayden's question in his head. Then, he smiled.

"One thing that I like about Matilda," Elijah said, as he brought his knife to eye level, "is that she never asks questions. She just does it."

"Why did you kill Grace?" Jayden asked as Elijah took a small step forward. Jayden took an equal step backwards.

"Kill her?" Elijah said, his head cocking to the other side. His cold, gray eyes lingered on me for a moment, and Jayden tried to move me out of his line of vision. Elijah smirked.

"Grace was always a lovely creature. She trusted me wholeheartedly. It had been a while since a girl had trusted me completely, with all their heart. Grace would do anything that I would ask of her," Elijah said, running a finger lightly down the edge of his knife. He smiled up at Jayden, but his eyes remained dead.

"Unfortunately, you just wouldn't leave her alone," Elijah said, his smile disappearing. "So, I had to help her."

"Why didn't you just kill me instead?" Jayden asked. "Wouldn't that have eliminated the problem?" Elijah gestured towards me.

"I wanted her with *me* forever. But, look at her. She's a spirit, attached to *you*. I thought she trusted me the most, but it turns out I was wrong," Elijah said, almost muttering the last part. Jayden's facade faltered.

"What do you mean?" he asked, asking a question that he truly wanted to know, not just trying to get a confession.

"I've killed before," Elijah said, nonchalantly. "Her spirit attached itself to me. Spirits seem to do that, if they feel wronged. Attach themselves to something, or someone. I took Grace's body in hopes that she would attach herself to it, but—"

"How do you know it's because they trusted you? She might've thought you killed her," Jayden said, almost indignant. Elijah stared at Jayden for a moment, and then burst into laughter, remembering my earlier words.

"She thought *you* killed her," he said. Jayden stiffened at his words. "She thought that was the reason why you two were attached. Loyal to the very end, I see." I spit in his direction.

"It's just my own defense mechanism," I said. "It had nothing to do with you." Elijah's eyes glinted with glee as he stared at me.

"But who cultivated that defense mechanism, Grace?" he said. His face looked like it was getting drunk off of the idea that I was still deluded by his teachings. It frightened me. This wasn't the therapist that I knew, that I trusted. But, this was what was hiding underneath that mask all along.

"Enough talking," Elijah said, his face relaxing. "Once you're gone, Grace will attach herself to me, like she should've in the first place." His face morphed into this terrifying expression of anger and fury before he lunged towards Jayden. Jayden dodged, and pulled me along as if the knife would've gone through me, too.

"Don't worry about me," I told him as Elijah tried to stab Jayden again. It narrowly missed his chest, and instead cut open his arm. I felt myself scream out at the action. Jayden looked up at me, and I realized that I distracted him as the knife went through his shoulder. Jayden fell to the ground in pain, as Elijah pulled out the knife. He pinned Jayden down and there was nothing I could do. Hot tears ran down the sides of my face as I screamed, as loud as I possibly could.

It was almost unworldly, the scream that came out of me. The windows around us shattered, the pieces slicing through Elijah's skin. He winced in pain, but he wouldn't move from his position. But, he was distracted long enough that Jayden was able to push him off before the knife came barreling towards his chest. Jayden tried to quickly stand up, but Elijah was quicker. He immediately jumped onto Jayden's back and even though Jayden tried to shake him off, Elijah was able to stab him again. Though, it didn't go as deep as the first stab wound. Jayden cried out in pain and I rushed to his side. Blood, Jayden's blood, was everywhere.

"Jayden, I'm so sorry. I'm so, so sorry," I said over and over again, like some kind of chant of atonement.

"Shut up," Elijah said, glaring at me. "You'll get over him. I'll make sure of it." I glared up at him. I knew I couldn't do anything to him. I would just go right through him. All I could do was distract him.

"He always hurt you, Grace," Elijah said, his voice almost buttery. "Boys say anything to hurt others. But I'm the exception."

"You're the only one who hurt me, Elijah," I said, using his first name. An eyebrow of his raised. It was clear he preferred to have the power of being my doctor over me.

"Why? Because you're dead?" he asked. He laughed, shaking his bloody knife at me. "I did you a favor. You can't be hurt anymore."

"Grace," Jayden's voice croaked out from underneath him. Elijah remembered that Jayden was alive and pulled his arm back to stab him in the back once more. Suddenly, sirens were heard and they were coming closer and closer. I watched as Elijah's usually calm, calculating gray eyes turned into panic and confusion.

"You called the cops?" Elijah said, his voice almost shrill. This gave Jayden enough distraction to use the rest of his energy to throw Elijah off of his back. He stood up, grabbed my hand, and ran towards the front door, a trail of blood following after him.

I knew that every part of Jayden wanted to go back and punch Elijah across the mouth, like he did with Allen so many years ago, but he wasn't strong enough to do so. All the hope he had in keeping his promise to me of not dying was to get help from the police. He threw open the front door and ran outside, just as the police pulled up. Their sirens were blaring and some officers ran towards Jayden, throwing him to the ground and cuffing him, as if he were the dangerous one.

"He's bleeding," I cried out, even though none of them could hear me. "He's going to die, please. Someone get him help, please, I'm begging you!" I sobbed in front of the cop who was putting Jayden's arms behind his back, cuffing his hands together. But, he couldn't see me.

"It's okay, Grace. I'm fine," Jayden muttered, his voice hoarse and his breath halting. He wasn't fine. I knew he wasn't fine in the slightest.

"Wait," one cop said. It was Mustache Man from when Jayden found my body. "Isn't that Jayden King?" I watched as Will's beat up mini van pulled up. He ran out, his eyes wide from the shock of seeing Jayden on the grass with his blood pouring out.

"That's Jayden King," Mustache Man confirmed after getting his phone out. "I took a picture with this guy. Get those cuffs off of him." The other cop agreed and Jayden tried to sit up, but he couldn't move the arm where he got stabbed in the shoulder.

"Elijah Adler," Jayden panted from the pain, "He killed Grace. He admitted it. We have the recording." His voice was short, breathing heavily between every word. Fortunately, the ambulance was driving up the street towards us.

"You did good, son," the cop said, putting a hand on Jayden's good shoulder. "Let's get you fixed up." He hoisted Jayden up as the EMTs ran out to grab him. I followed after Jayden, but I could hear Will talking frantically to the cop as he gave them the recording.

"He also has her body. It's upstairs in a weird closet thing, hidden in the walls," I heard Will say. I watched as Elijah Adler was led out of his house in handcuffs, his gray eyes staring intensely at me. I quickly turned to look at Jayden as I floated through the ambulance doors. I wasn't going to waste another minute thinking about Elijah. I was done letting him creep his way into my thoughts. I was done letting him manipulate me. The sirens turned on, and the ambulance drove at the speed of light towards the nearest hospital.

twenty-eight

I HELD Jayden's hand through all of it. I wasn't sure if he knew I was there or not at times. But, it wasn't until hours later in the hospital did he wake up again. He groaned as his eyes slowly opened, his gaze taking me in.

"You're still here," he managed to say. I tried to smile. I knew what he meant. The wrong had been righted, Elijah Adler was arrested for murdering me. My spirit should be able to cross now. I shrugged, though I saw the string that held me to Jayden slowly start to fade.

"I didn't want to leave until you were okay," I muttered. He scooted over in his hospital bed, the movement causing him to wince, so that I could lay down next to him. I gingerly laid down on my side, facing him.

"Your dad was here," I said. He scoffed at my words.

"My dad? He wouldn't care if I died," he responded.

"He does care," I said, remembering how his dad was in the hospital. He and Jayden's mom were distraught at the sight of their son.

"My dad came here, too," I said. Jayden looked at me, trying to gauge my expression.

"Why?" he eventually asked, after figuring out that it was okay to ask.

"He came to thank you and he thanked your parents for raising you the way that they did," I said. I remembered how my dad bowed to Mr. and Mrs. King.

"Thank you for raising a son who loved my daughter enough to do this," my father had said to them. "He'll always be her hero." Even my dad knew before I ever did that I had loved Jayden with a fierceness.

"Your daughter never needed a hero," is all that Mr. King said in response to my father.

"I have no doubt that she guided our son and protected him through it all," Mrs. King said, as she held Jayden's hand. His other hand was gripping mine tightly, even though he was unconscious. Protected him? I wish her words were true, and a feeling of guilt rose into my chest and refused to leave after hearing her words. I couldn't do anything to stop what had happened. And it was my fault in the first place.

"What happened isn't your fault," Jayden said, interrupting my thoughts. How he was able to read my mind, I wasn't sure.

"Why did you like me?" I asked, as I saw the string start to fade more. I didn't have much time left with Jayden, and I could feel my heart cry out in pain at the realization. Jayden brushed a lock of black hair from my face, his eyes the warmest I've ever seen them, holding the sun within them.

"Because you're the most interesting person I've ever met," he simply said.

"But, you like girly girls," I said. "I've never been a girly girl." He laughed at those words.

"You really don't know yourself, huh?" he said. "You *are* a girly girl. Through and through. I could just see that you were insecure. Since the first day I saw you, you were just trying to hide yourself. But, I saw you, you know. A lot of people saw you." I blinked as I stared at him, memorizing his face. I could tell that he was doing the same thing.

"We don't have a lot of time left," I muttered as he put his hand on my cheek. He squinted from the pain —or from the realization, I wasn't sure which.

"I know," he said.

"I think I've always loved you," I murmured into his hand. He smiled slightly, a twinkle in his eye.

"I knew that, too," he said. He closed his eyes as he said, "I thought we would have more time. Will always told me to just tell you, but... I thought we had our whole lives." He opened them again, his eyes reminding me of him as a twelve-year-old boy playing video games with Will.

"We did have a lifetime together," I said, the threat

of tears thickening my voice. "My lifetime."

"Shyla *did* think we were dating the whole time anyways," Jayden said, a smile playing on his lips. I laughed and then I watched as his face fell.

"I don't want to live a life without you," he whispered. "I don't even remember what life was like before you."

"Well, me cutting you off should be enough practice," I chuckled. He rolled his eyes.

"Seriously, G, I don't know what I'll do without you," he said. I smiled and held his face in my hands.

"You're going to be the next legendary basketball player, you'll meet someone like Mia—because only someone like her can handle you—and start a family with them, and you'll live until you're over a hundred years old," I said, almost like a prayer. "And when the time comes, I'll be there, waiting. It'll feel like no time has passed at all." I didn't know if there was an afterlife, if I would really be waiting somewhere for him or not. But, I just wanted to give him any comfort that I could.

"I can't move on from you," he said. "Not after…" I felt my heart stop. Will was right. I shouldn't have let it get this far.

"I'm sorry, Jayden," I said. I would have to apologize to him for a hundred lifetimes for the pain of loss that he was going to have to live with.

"I should've ignored you for longer," Jayden said, smiling. "Should've just let you be an annoying ghost by my side for years."

"He would've killed someone else though," I pointed out, "Eventually." Jayden nodded, almost dejected. It was as if the sun that always surrounded him was starting to fade. At least I got to experience it, his sun, for a little while.

"Don't let my death be a burden to you, Jayden," I whispered.

"I just have so many regrets," he muttered, his eyes gazing into the very depths of my soul. Hearing his mother start to come back down the hallway, I touched his lips before I kissed them, hoping to imprint some part of me onto his body. Hoping that he'll someday say my name with the same intimacy that he had said Mia's. The only way I would live on would be through his memories. And I knew that was selfish of me. Perhaps this whole time I was being selfish. But if I was, I would be until the very end.

"I love you, Jayden," I said, as I pulled away. "Arguing with you were honestly the best moments of my life." I smiled, as I saw the last of the string fade away. I watched as his eyes widened at my disappearing form and could hear the guttural sobs that came after his mother rushed into the room. But, in the end, all I saw was darkness. My last thoughts were a reassurance, to myself and maybe to him: In the end, someday down the line, he'll be *fine*.

THE END.

Bianca K. Gray wrote the fantasy novel The Celestials and graduated from the University of Virginia with a Bachelor degree in English and a Master degree in English Education. Bianca has always had a love for literature that she wants others to discover and cultivate within themselves. She currently resides in the *sometimes* sunny San Francisco, CA with her fiancé, rambunctious shih-tzu, and the most adorably kitty cat.

instagram.com/biancakgray.author